Guns for
General Washington

Books by Fairfax Downey

GUNS FOR GENERAL WASHINGTON

FAMOUS HORSES OF THE CIVIL WAR

GENERAL CROOK, INDIAN FIGHTER

MASCOTS

THE SHINING FILLY

A HORSE FOR GENERAL LEE

TRAIL OF THE IRON HORSE

FREE AND EASY

CATS OF DESTINY

DOGS OF DESTINY

HORSES OF DESTINY

THE SEVENTH'S STAGHOUND

CAVALRY MOUNT

ARMY MULE

JEZEBEL THE JEEP

DOG OF WAR

WAR HORSE

Guns for
General Washington

by Fairfax Downey

DRAWINGS BY LEONARD VOSBURGH

THOMAS NELSON & SONS

Edinburgh   NEW YORK   *Toronto*

Library of Congress Catalog Card Number: 61-13828

PRINTED IN THE UNITED STATES OF AMERICA

To Guns I Have Served
    U.S. 3-inch
    French 75-mm.
    U.S. 105-mm. howitzer

Contents

Contents

Chapter I

The Guns Are Named

THE black muzzles of the three brass cannon gaped across Boston Common. Crews stood alertly at their posts around them, the bombardiers holding glowing linstock matches over the vents. Loaded with blank cartridges for a drill though they were, there was no mistaking the menace of these guns. If their like had been charged with grapeshot and manned by British Regulars one evening in 1770, five years ago, many more would have died than the five citizens cut down by musketry in the riot Bostonians called the "Massacre."

Dark-haired Second Lieutenant Kent Andrews, of the crack Boston Grenadier Corps' artillery train, swept the line of guns with his keen gray eyes. Their polished barrels, embossed with the arms of the Province of Massachusetts, glistened in the sunlight. Lieutenant Andrews was proud to serve with these trim three-pounders, so called from the weight of the cannon balls they fired.

Andrews, the handsome uniform of the Corps setting off his tall, well-built figure, faced about and saluted his superior officer. "Ready to fire, sir," he reported.

A huge man, towering over all the matrosses, or cannoneers, who had to be at least five feet ten inches in height, stepped forward and returned the salute. First Lieutenant Henry Knox was light on his feet for all the two hundred and fifty pounds on his six-foot-three frame.

"Fire from the right. Two rounds," Knox ordered.

Andrews shouted, "Man pieces! Number One, fire!"

The first bombardier touched his match to the vent priming as he quickly moved one pace to the right, clear of the wheels. His gun flashed, its blank charge bellowing. Like a live thing, it bucked and sprang backward in recoil. Number One's crew jumped to grasp its wheels and roll it forward into position. An artilleryman thrust a rod tipped with an oversized corkscrew, called a worm, into the bore, withdrawing the smoldering remnants of the paper cartridge. Another dipped his sponge staff in a water bucket, swabbed and cooled the bore. Hardly had he finished when a third matross was at the muzzle with a fresh charge and wad to be rammed in, while a fourth stopped the vent. He covered it with the leather-protected palm of his left hand to prevent any fiery powder particle remaining in the tube from exploding the new load.

At one-minute intervals the other two cannon spoke in turn, and again spurts of flame ran along the line. Knox took approving note of the conduct of firing, smooth as clockwork. These guns, well served, would be deadly in action, deadlier than a musket volley and with better than eight times the small arms' range of fifty yards. Through his mind ran the still rankling memory of the "Massacre" which he himself had vainly tried to prevent, begging the British officer in command to restrain his troops' itching trigger fingers. Would there be more such trouble? There were signs of it. If any fighting took place, there was reassurance in the fact that these three-pounders were so well handled by men who, though British subjects, were beginning to call themselves Americans.

Dismissing these thoughts, Knox sharply ordered, "Cease firing!" The squads resumed their posts at attention.

One of a pair of British officers, observing the drill, turned to the other to ask, "Smartly done for provincial militia, wouldn't you say?"

The second, an artilleryman newly arrived from England, answered ungrudgingly, "Smartly done even for Regulars. I suppose the Royal Artillery handled their training, Major?"

"In part only. Most of the credit's due to their commander—the hulking chap yonder."

"Knox? But I'm told he's a book-seller."

"So he is, and so's his second lieutenant, an assistant in his shop. The London Book Store. I suggest you visit it. It lives up to its name. It's well stocked with the latest books from home."

"But a bookish artillerist!"

"Just so. And an engineer, too. Knox carries standard works on the military art, not only in English but in French and German. He stocks Robins' *New Principles of Gunnery* and even Müller's *Treatise of Artillery*. What's more he has them at his finger tips—nor does it matter that he lacks a couple of those. Notice that silk handkerchief wrapped around his left hand? It conceals the loss of two fingers, mangled when his fowling piece burst while duck hunting."

"We'd best think about our own fingers getting burned." The newcomer from England had turned grave. "These Bostonians are giving us trouble, aren't they? Every ship seems to be bringing over more troops for our garrison."

"Yes, they stir up a fuss here from time to time, about the tea taxes and such. Two years ago a gang of young rascals, disguised as Indians, raided a merchant ship and threw every chest of tea aboard into the harbor. Same thing happened in New York. Then five years ago a mob here attacked our sentries who were forced to fire and kill a few of the rioters. It was called a 'massacre' by self-styled 'patriots' among the townsfolk.

"But we needn't be unduly concerned. I doubt if it ever comes to rebellion. If it does, General Gage will cope with it. Shopkeepers, artisans, and farmers won't stand up against Regulars. If they try, a volley or two of musketry or a whiff of grapeshot from your guns will send them packing."

The artilleryman soberly nodded toward the three-pounders. "What if our fire were returned by those guns, as ably handled as we've seen them this morning?"

"Not likely." The major waved the possibility aside. "It's true there's some question of Knox's loyalty and his men's. But they'd have no guns to serve. If the unrest and rebellious mutterings hereabouts increase"—the speaker lowered his voice—"Gage plans to seize the arms of the militia and any that may be stored in the villages around Boston."

The other nodded confidently, and the two officers walked over to congratulate Knox on his drill. When they left, Andrews asked his commander, "Shall I return the battery to the gun-house, sir?"

"Do so." Andrews spoke to a big sergeant. Rapidly the crews executed his orders. Ammunition side-boxes were replaced on the gun carriages, and ropes fastened to the trails. "Dragropes! March!". . . . "Take care to wheel by the right!" The column of cannon was hauled away.

"Our guns," Knox declared proudly, watching them roll off. "Cast in England from old cannon sent over by the General Court of Massachusetts. I've a mind to name them, Kent."

"Name them? Should guns bear names, sir?"

"Of course. Since early days they've been duly and properly christened. Many have borne the names of kings and queens. Louis XII named a dozen huge pieces after the twelve peers of France. Charles V piously called his heaviest battery, which he used against the infidel Turk, 'The Twelve Apostles.'"

"I'd not like to have been in the gun crew that manned 'Judas.'"

"Nor I. It probably blew up in their faces. Then there was the mighty bombard named Mad Meg, the Great Gun of Ghent. Meg's calibre was twenty-five inches; she was ten feet long and threw a 600-pound ball. Others were called 'Invincible,' 'Thunder and Fury,' and 'The Organist.' There was a particularly deadly cannon which I've always thought its crew must have named because some of them had been roughly treated by the regimental surgeon. They dubbed it 'The Doctor.'"

Knox laughed, and went on. "Not only were the names of those guns of olden days often embossed on their barrels but their prowess was proclaimed there as well. A legend on one, mounted on the Rhine fortress of the warlike

Bishop of Treves, boasted: 'I am called the Griffin. I serve my lord of Treves. Where he commands me to exert my strength, I straightway throw down gates and walls.'

"We ought to continue the custom," the big man said. "To me, a cannon worth the serving is an individual. It has a personality. Have you noticed how our Number One piece booms? Sonorously and somewhat pompously. I hereby name it 'John Hancock' after our revered and able, though self-important, patriot leader."

Andrews grinned. "And Number Two, sir?"

"Its voice is assertive, too," Knox said. "Yet it speaks more sharply and succinctly, with fewer rolling periods in its discourse when it chimes into a salvo. Here and now I make it the namesake of our estimable John Adams."

"Shall we name Number Three for Samuel Adams?" Andrews suggested.

Knox shook his head. "Not yet, not now. Sam, for all his boldness and energy in our cause, has a touch of the demagogue. I am not certain that his bark is not worse than his bite. That must never be said of any cannon of ours. The day may come soon when Number Three fires round shot, and none must mistake it for a blank charge. Let it stay nameless for the time being."

Big Sergeant Sampson, almost as hefty a man as Knox, returned to salute and report, "Battery secure in the gun-house, sir."

"Very good, Sergeant. Dismiss."

When the non-commissioned officer had gone, Knox said quietly, "Secure? I'm none too sure of that. From what I hear, King George's men have their eyes on those guns and our other arms. On the powder and ball we have at Concord and Lexington, too. They don't altogether trust us."

Andrews' eyes snapped with excitement. "Do you think it might come to fighting, sir?" he asked.

"Not if the King's ministers listen to reason. Not unless they and the Royal Governor and the Tories stir up Gage, who thinks us meek, to some rash action. But they may . . . they may. I'd not put it past them. Keep your ears open when we dine with the Royal Welch Fusiliers tonight, Kent. Wine loosens tongues. They are our friends, gallant gentlemen—they and most of the other British officers—but at any moment they may turn into enemies."

Andrews, bristling, burst out, "If they dare seize our guns—"

A smile spread across Henry Knox's broad, ruddy face. "The guns," he finished, "will not be there to be seized."

Scores of candles in wall sconces and on the long banquet table gaily illuminated the mess hall of the Royal Welch Fusiliers. This was a festive occasion—Saint David's Day, March 1st—an anniversary when the sons of Wales, wherever they are, honor their patron saint.

Henry Knox and Kent Andrews beamed across the board at each other. It was a signal favor for officers of American Colonial troops to be guests of a famous regiment at its gala evening. Knox's small gray eyes twinkled as he joked with his table-mates. It's no wonder, Andrews thought, that the Royal Welch and the other British like Henry Knox. He's only four years older than my twenty-one, but even their senior officers admire his ability as a soldier.

The big American was holding forth on his hobby, the guns. "I grant you that infantry deserves its title of 'Queen of Battles,'" he declared. "So the Royal Welch have valiantly proved on many a field. But give me the artillery, gentlemen. It opens the way for you of the foot—or bars it. Which would you rather face? Charging cavalry, which cannot break your squares, or a volley from well-served cannon?"

A veteran major of Fusiliers smiled. "It's all one to infantry, Mister Knox—emptying saddles or picking off gunners. That is, if your precious cannon haven't blown up and wiped out their crews for us."

"Your small arms have been known to do the same." Knox held up his silk-wrapped left hand. "Keep your muskets. I'll take the guns that far outrange them. Give me the howitzers and the mortars that force a besieged town to surrender."

Several of the Britons looked thoughtful. Siege guns undeniably did that. If talk of rebellion by the Colonies came to action, cannon on the heights above Boston could force the evacuation of its garrison. But of course the Americans had no big guns—nothing larger than the small ordnance in the artillery train of the militia.

Andrews, listening intently, sensed the veiled warning his chief was uttering. Knox was actually letting his hosts understand that someday he might be trading in cannon balls instead of books. There was something magnificent about such effrontery. A provincial militiaman challenging His Majesty's Regulars—politely but boldly throwing down the gauntlet before a noted regiment like the Royal Welch Fusiliers, with nearly a hundred years of glorious history behind it and the names of such mighty victories as Namur, Fontenoy, and Minden blazoned on its record. Yet Andrews never doubted that his chief meant everything he said and implied, or that he lacked the courage to back up his words. After all, if Great Britain continued to suppress its Colonies' liberties, to heap unjust taxes on them and deny them representation in Parliament, what could an American of spirit do but rise in defense of his freedom and his rights?

A voice from Andrews' left rallied him on his serious expression.

"No long faces, Kent Andrews. Not on Saint David's Day," chided a good-looking young officer of Fusiliers. "Neither our patron on his anniversary nor I, his namesake, can countenance any gloom tonight."

"Sorry." Andrews smiled at Ensign David Thorpe, a friend he would be most reluctant to fight if the dispute between Britain and America broke out of bounds.

"The time of toasts and ceremony approaches," Thorpe told him. "You must be prepared. Soon a leek will be passed to you."

"A leek?" Andrews asked.

"The revered national vegetable of Wales. The onion is its humble relation. Fortunately we found a Welshman in Dorchester who grows leeks in his garden. Otherwise we must have brought them over, dried and withered, by ship. Without leeks Saint David cannot be properly honored. Eating them tonight is a regimental tradition of ours. So is our spelling of Welch the old way—with a 'c' instead of an 's'. And this flash." He reached over his shoulder to touch a cluster of black ribbons beneath the collar of his tunic. "They say the flash was originally attached to protect coats from powder on our queues, or perhaps it's a survival of the ribbon that once bound the queues.

"Another tradition is Toby Purcell's spurs. He was second in command when our colonel was killed at the Battle of Boyne in 1690. Lieutenant Colonel Purcell took over and led with such gallantry that the regiment has always kept his spurs. They will be brought out, exhibited, and toasted tonight.

"But I've gotten away from leeks. I see my fellow officers are instructing Mister Knox about them. Now here's what you do when the toast is proposed—"

Thorpe had not finished speaking when the Colonel of the Fusiliers called for the ceremony. Drums rolled outside the mess hall, and fifes shrilled a lively air.

" 'Of Noble Race was Shenkin' " Thorpe identified the tune. "It's always played on this occasion."

"Who was Shenkin?" Andrews asked.

"Nobody seems to know. A Welsh hero of olden times, I guess."

Through doors flung wide marched a vivid procession. Andrews saw that it was headed by a white goat, the famous mascot of the Royal Welch, led by a tall Fusilier, the Goat-Major. The animal was a beauty, his long coat washed to snowy whiteness, his curved horns gilded. On his forehead he wore a silver plaque, engraved with the name and crown of George III, his donor; his back was covered with an embroidered blanket, as splendidly scarlet as his regiment's uniform. For the Royal Welch he was the present pet in a long line of mascots, always white goats named Billy.

After the goat and his attendant strode a tall drum-major, towering higher still in a big bearskin cap with gleaming front plate and white tassels, and small drummer boys and fifers, playing lustily. The mess sergeant followed with a platter of leeks which he offered first to each newly joined officer and guest. Knox and Andrews took theirs, stood on their chairs, as instructed, and munched the pungent vegetable. Each quaffed from a loving cup and spoke the toast, "And Saint David."

After Billy, his guardian, and his music completed their march around the long table, they halted and, according to custom, one of the drummer boys unslung his drum and mounted on the goat's back. But that was a tradition to which Billy refused to subscribe tonight. He uttered a loud, indignant bleat, bucked violently, and threw his rider. Up on the table he leaped, smashing cups and crockery. He butted a stout captain who tried to catch him. A flash of white, and Billy was out the window, vainly pursued by the Goat-Major and musicians and cheered enthusiastically in his flight through the streets by gleeful citizens.

Knox, roaring with laughter, watched the goat vanish. Then he turned to his lieutenant and, glancing at the British uniforms around them, said softly with an undertone of seriousness:

"It seems that Boston—in more ways than one—has got the King's goat."

Chapter II

Save the Guns!

THERE was tension in the air of Boston in mid-April, 1775. Townsfolk felt their skins tingle as they walked through the streets. Their uneasiness increased when they passed British soldiers, some striding with military stiffness, others with a blustering swagger. Small boys made faces at their backs, but their elders watched them warily. Though the Redcoats were unarmed, their hands could grasp loaded, bayoneted muskets quickly enough, as they had before. Bostonians sensed the same sort of trouble impending now that they remembered from that bloody evening they called the "Massacre."

The usually sedate atmosphere of Henry Knox's London Book-Store on Cornhill had vanished. Customers, who came to chat as they browsed, spoke carefully and eyed each other suspiciously. Tories, deeply loyal to the King, looked askance at those who termed themselves patriots; they were rebels at heart, in the opinion of the loyalists. Plainly they did not trust that tall young woman, Lucy Flucker Knox, the proprietor's bride, though her parents were ardent Tories. It was known she had defied them to marry the book-seller and was as apt to turn against the King as he.

Lucy did not stay long in the shop today. Icily polite to the Tory ladies, she swept out like a full-rigged ship under sail. The backward glance she gave her husband was full of anxiety. If the trouble everyone was expecting ended in fighting, Henry Knox would surely be in the thick of it.

Kent Andrews finished selling a book to a customer and went forward to greet a new arrival, a favorite of Lucy Knox's and certainly no less of his own. Constancy Waite, her eyes as blue as the cornflowers in the pattern of her muslin gown, smiled at him. Yellow curls tossed under her pert cap as she hurried up to him.

"I shouldn't bother you here, Kent," the girl apologized, "but I had to tell you we found the Royal Welch's lost billy goat in our yard. He was mightily taken with our nanny goat, and she with him, and he would not leave. I sent word to the regiment, and the handsomest ensign came for him."

"By any chance David Thorpe?"

"Oh, yes. You know him? Isn't he nice? He asked leave to call again and tender the regiment's thanks."

Andrews answered: "I had meant to present him to you myself someday." But he hadn't. There was no point in introducing a good-looking rival to your girl. He could not help feeling a twinge of jealousy as, Constancy tripped out of the bookstore.

Knox noted it in his frown and said with a chuckle, "Never mind, Kent. We have other matters in hand." The shop had emptied, but he spoke softly. "I've had a warning."

"From whom, sir?"

"Paul Revere, no less. A moment ago we talked in the back of the shop. He's learned from spies for our Committee for Public Safety that General Gage may act any day now. Paul himself has been riding south as a courier. To Connecticut, New York, on to Philadelphia. They are with us. There are assurances from Virginia and the other southern provinces, too, that what we hardly dared hope may happen—that if conflict comes, all the Colonies will stand together."

"Massachusetts can stand alone!" Andrews exclaimed fervently.

Knox shook his head, and asked gently, "Against the might of Great Britain? Listen carefully now," he went on, his voice grave. "Revere says Gage is planning to seize our leaders and our stores of arms. Paul is watching over John Hancock and John Adams and our arms and powder at Lexington and Concord."

Andrews spoke suddenly. "There are arms even closer to home that will bear watching, sir."

"Precisely, Kent. Our cannon. Our battery commander, Captain Paddock, Tory that he is, would turn them over to the British at the drop of a hat. Our guns, 'Hancock' and 'Adams,' are in as serious danger as their namesakes—along with our third piece, as yet unnamed."

"I have a name to propose for it, sir. Let's call it 'Mistress Lucy,' after your lady wife."

Knox grinned appreciatively. " 'Mistress Lucy' it is," he declared. "And now, Lieutenant Andrews, you will don uniform, and proceed straightway to our gun-house and see to the safety of my wifely cannon and the others. Make haste, Kent! Even now we may be too late."

Kent Andrews, in uniform, strode down West Street and went through a gate in the high fence that enclosed both the gun-house and a schoolhouse. He halted and stood staring along with the group of curious and excited children who had just streamed into the yard from the last class of the afternoon. Before the locked door of the gun-house paced a British sentry. Knox's fears had been justified. It was too late.

A scowl creased a deep cleft between the American's eyes, as he walked up and gruffly demanded, "Sentry, why are you posted here?"

The soldier, a Royal Welch Fusilier, presented arms in salute, then brought his musket to port, barring the way, and answered, "Guard over the guns, sir. They're not to be taken out without a permit from Headquarters."

"But they're our guns. I'm an officer of the Boston artillery."

"I know you are, sir, but them's my orders."

So it had come, as Paul Revere warned. Gage had seized the guns. While Andrews hesitated in angry confusion, a detail marched up to relieve the sentinel, and the whole affair became still more infuriating. Ensign Thorpe was acting as officer of the guard.

"Bothered about something, Leftenant Andrews?" Thorpe did not try to hide his amusement at the other's discomfiture.

"At least some explanation would seem due for this," Andrews answered stiffly, gesturing toward the guarded gun-house.

"Certainly. It's General Gage's orders. Isn't that enough?"

"Not by any means. By whose authority does your General deny troops of the Province of Massachuetts exercise with their own arms?"

"By authority vested in him by the Crown—if he chose to deny you. But he doesn't forbid your legitimate use of your guns. Obtain a permit and you may take out your little cannon and drill with them, providing that you do so under an infantry escort, which we'll be happy to furnish."

Andrews, unable to curb his temper, burst out: "You mean to say we can't use our own cannon without your mounting guard on us?"

"Mounting guard? Oh, I shouldn't call it that. Hasn't artillery always needed infantry to protect it and keep it from losing its guns?"

With a derisive smile, Thorpe spoke to his sergeant, and the detail marched off.

Andrews, casting a bitter look at the new sentry, stepped over to the schoolmaster, who had shooed his pupils homeward and was watching from the doorway. Abraham Holbrook, a stanch patriot, spoke quietly.

"We expected this, Kent; but we were caught napping."

"Someone else is going to be caught napping." Andrews jerked his head slightly toward the sentry. "We're not letting the Lobster-backs impound our guns! Could you arrange to be working late in the schoolhouse some evening soon, Abraham? Myself and four stout fellows will stop by—"

"For a scholarly discussion of course."

"Of course. It will wax so hot we'll have to appeal the argument to the sentry. In case he does not understand, we may have to—"

"—to pound it into his thick skull."

"Just so. And while he's pondering it—"

"*Exeunt* three cannon," the schoolmaster added.

"An exit without alarums and excursions—except an excursion out of Boston. We may have great need of those guns."

"Henry Knox approves?"

"Completely. He'd already planned it. But we must manage it without him. I'm sure he's being watched, and the British won't permit him to leave Boston. Give me time, Abraham, to make sure of a good hiding place in the country for the guns. Be ready for us three nights from tonight."

But again the patriots had delayed too long. The appointed date could not have been more unfortunately chosen. It was April 18, 1775.

CHAPTER III

Rescue

Т HAT evening all Boston was aware that something was afoot in the British garrison. Sentries had been doubled. Troops evidently had been confined to barracks, for the usual throngs of soldiers failed to fill the taverns. British officers in pairs purposefully patrolled the streets. Clamping down a curfew, they halted and questioned any townsfolk who were abroad. All were ordered back to their homes unless they could convince the patrols that they were on emergency errands. The strictest prohibition was enforced against any Bostonian, even a Loyalist, leaving town.

Andrews, Sergeant Sampson, and three men of the artillery train barely managed to dodge the patrols and reach

26

the yard on West Street soon after dusk. To their dismay, a glance through the open gate revealed two sentinels, instead of one, on guard, bayonets fixed, in front of the gunhouse. Andrews whispered an order. His men followed him to the rear fence which they scaled, and slipped through the back door of the schoolhouse where the anxious Holbrook was awaiting them.

The undertaking had grown desperate, the Americans agreed, but still it must be risked. In all events they were six to two. When the darkness thickened, three of them, creeping around the sides of the gun-house, would rush up and overpower each sentry. They would have to be swift and sudden. One shot fired, and the alarm would be given.

"Some of us may take a bayonet thrust," Andrews said softly, "but we must get those muskets away from them at all costs."

"Grab for their powder pans," Sergeant Sampson growled. "Get a hand under the hammer, and small good it'll do 'em to pull the trigger."

"Small good it'll do our hands either," a young artilleryman said with a chuckle, "but anything in a pinch."

Andrews frowned at him but said nothing. Young Ephraim Brooks was always cracking jokes—he didn't seem to take anything seriously—but he was a good gunner nevertheless. Maybe it was well in a crisis to have a lighthearted lad around, keeping the rest of the men from growing overtense.

But Sergeant Sampson, in whose book flippancy was bad for discipline, snapped at the joker, "Shut your trap, Brooks."

"Aw, Sergeant," the gunner protested. "Us Brooks, we got to babble. It's our nature. You know. Babbling brooks."

Grinning, he dodged a cuff from the non-com's heavy hand.

Minutes dragged by. Andrews waited nervously and with deepening despair. What miserable luck! Even if they succeeded in disposing of the sentries, the odds were against their getting the guns out of Boston, with the streets being patrolled and most of the exits probably closed. Three guns to be moved, with only two men on the dragropes of each. True, Andrews had allowed for that, and some of his artillerymen, dressed as farmers, were to be waiting with teams of horses. Could they possibly be at the meeting place now? It was all too likely that they had been rounded up and sent home under guard. No matter. That risk, too, must be run.

The lieutenant looked through the schoolhouse's shuttered windows. "All right, it's dark enough," he said, and moved toward the back door.

Outside a sentry challenged sharply, and the Americans froze as they listened in consternation. A woman's voice answered. The guard was heard to say, "Pass then, ma'am. Try the schoolhouse."

Constancy Waite found Andrews in the other building and sighed with relief. "Kent, I've only a minute," she whispered. "I said Mother is sick, and I'm looking for a doctor. David Thorpe stopped me on my way, and I told my fib to him. He would have come with me, but luckily he was on duty. I've a message from Henry Knox. He says the British have barred every way out of Boston. It's hopeless to get the guns out tonight. They may seize them tomorrow, but that chance must be taken. Their loss is certain if you move them out of here tonight. I must go now. Good-by."

"Thank you, Constancy. You're brave and true." Andrews took the girl's hand and kissed it before them all. She blushed, and ran out into the night.

So she had outwitted Thorpe, Andrews reflected elatedly. It was wonderful to know she had never wavered from the patriot cause. Doubts he had been unable to dismiss had been bothering him for weeks. There were too many Boston girls, not all Tories either, who kept company with dashing British officers—girls who were likely to follow their hearts, regardless of politics. Constancy obviously had disliked deceiving David Thorpe, yet she had not hesitated.

Andrews pulled his mind back to the distressing fact that the coup he had planned so carefully was ruined by Constancy's news. His men had sunk back on their benches and were regarding him gloomily, as he racked his brain for an alternative. At last Abraham Holbrook broke the heavy silence.

"I'm no artilleryman," said the schoolmaster, "and this is scarce a matter of classical knowledge, but I believe guns are more important than gun carriages."

"You're right," Andrews said. "Carpenters and wheelwrights can quickly build us carriages. Casting cannon is another matter. But we'd be caught carrying the guns through the streets as quickly as rolling them."

"Postpone that journey. The best hiding place is often near at hand."

"What do you mean? Where?"

"Right here in the schoolhouse."

Sergeant Sampson grinned. "I should have gone to school longer. Seems a man learns something there after all. Now let's go reason with those sentries.

"No need of that." The schoolmaster spoke up again. "During recess I had some of my boys loosen two planks on the rear wall of the gun-house. The gap will be wide enough for the gun barrels to pass through, if they are taken off their carriages."

"Well devised, Abraham!" Andrews sighed with relief. "Come on now, men, and not a sound."

In the shadows behind the schoolhouse they pried away loosened boards. One plank creaked, and the Americans stiffened, pulses pounding, but the measured tread of the sentries did not alter. The raiders could thank their lucky stars for the British Army's rigid discipline. So many paces, a halt, face about, walk your post in the opposite direction, keeping always on the alert—those were guard duty orders. But in following them a sentry was apt to be too busy being smart and military to listen carefully.

The boards were off now, and a gap opened. Sergeant Sampson tried to wedge his big body through, and stuck. Just in time, Andrews clapped a hand over Eph Brooks' mouth to smother the titter he knew must be coming. They hauled the sergeant out, and the rest of them slipped into the gun-house, groping in the dark for the cannon. Fingers pulled out the trunnion keys and slid back the cap squares, and brawny arms lifted the cool brass tubes from their carriages.

Get them out now, quickly and quietly. Thank heaven the guns weren't twelve-pounders or even sixes. The three cannon were eased silently through the gap, but outside one of the carriers stumbled over a stone and half lost his hold. "Hancock" was about to slip from sweaty hands and thud to the ground when Sergeant Sampson stepped in and clutched it in a bear hug, supporting the gun's whole weight. After that near-betrayal they got the guns into the schoolhouse without mishap.

While the unsuspecting sentries mounted guard over

empty gun carriages, "Hancock," "Adams," and "Mistress Lucy" were safely concealed in the schoolroom beneath the teacher's platform.

The raiders, separating, made their way stealthily back to their homes. Andrews, before returning to his widowed mother's house, climbed the wall into the book-seller's garden where he found his senior officer waiting for him. Knox broke off his hearty congratulations on the success with the guns to peer upward through the darkness. A light shone suddenly in the belfry of the North Church.

"The signal!" the big man exclaimed. "Wait!"

A second beacon flashed out beside the first.

"By sea! They go by water!" Knox cried. "Then they'll debark on Charlestown Neck and march."

"'They'? I don't understand, sir."

"British troops. The Regulars are out! Off to Lexington to capture John Hancock and John Adams and our arms and stores there and at Concord. Now Revere can ride— and Prescott and Dawes—and give the alarm. If only our guns could be waiting to welcome the Lobster-backs! But the Minutemen will be ready for them."

Andrews poured out eager questions. "Will there be a fight? Can we get there? Can't we—?"

"Hold hard, Kent. The answer to your first is: I don't know. To your second: No, we can't get out of Boston tonight. But tomorrow—that may be a different story. We'll have to await events. Meanwhile here are your orders."

After listening carefully, Andrews gripped his superior's hand and climbed back over the garden wall.

Hurrying hoofbeats through the night. Urgent shouts of riders echoing in the streets of sleeping villages. "The Reg-

ulars are out!" Pounding hoofs behind and around the
couriers, as mounted British officers closed in and cut them
off. Dawes escaping, but Prescott and Revere captured,
and a grenadier sergeant riding off on the swift mare
Revere had borrowed from Mr. Larkin. Too late, General
Gage. Warning is given, the alarm spread.

Minutemen mustering around the green at Lexington.
An angry order branding them rebels and bidding them
break ranks and disperse. Muskets leveled along ranks,
terrible in scarlet, the hue soon matched by a flaming volley. Bodies in gray and brown homespun crumpled in the
fields.

The scarlet tide flows on across the bridge at Concord.
Again a crash of firearms, and now American muskets and
fowling pieces answer. Tall grenadiers topple, and the tide
ebbs slowly. Pent in, scourged by fire from behind stone
walls and fences, it ebbs faster. Blood-red now and broken,
it surges back toward the sea. Lord Percy and his column
marching to the rescue, with fifes impudently shrilling
Yankee Doodle, cannot stem it. They only swell it as it
carries its flotsam of wounded into Boston.

Late that same day a bulky man in civilian clothes
slipped out of town, accompanied by a tall young woman.
Henry Knox had wisely decided to put himself beyond the
reach of the British Army which had been pressing him to
accept a commission and serve against the Rebels. Lucy
walked by his side, holding her cloak carefully as they
passed the guard posts to keep her husband's sword, sewn
in its lining, from rattling.

Next evening a farm wagon, loaded with provisions,
drove into town. It was warmly welcomed, for already
Boston was under siege. With amazing speed a small

American army had concentrated at Cambridge: undaunted Minutemen of Massachusetts, determined to avenge their dead; resolute volunteers from New Hampshire, Connecticut, and Rhode Island. The wagon, emptied, was passed out readily and its driver urged to return soon with more food. He and another countryman on the seat beside him promised they would. Not until they were well past the last picket, did Kent Andrews turn to glance over his shoulder at the layer of straw on the wagon bed, straw which the British sentries had failed to examine. He spoke to his companion.

"We can go faster now, Jemmy. Jouncing won't bother our scholars back there."

"How do you mean 'scholars'?" the man asked.

"Our three cannon under the straw. They've been to school, haven't they?"

The driver laughed and clucked his horses into a trot. A muffled thudding and clanking came from the wagon bed as they rumbled into the American lines.

CHAPTER IV

Action on a Hill

CLOUDS of smoke, stabbed by flashes of flame, wreathed the gun ports of the British warships in Boston harbor. An instant later Kent Andrews' ears rang to the crashes of the broadsides. Again and again the big naval guns, far heavier than any that could be handled on a battlefield, thundered on from that dawn of June 17th, 1775. Their shells hurtled toward the new Rebel fortifications on the brow of Breed's Hill.

A feeling of weakness hamstrung Andrews' knees. He and his battery of the Massachusetts Regiment of Artillery were marching into that fire. From the pallor of faces around him he judged he had turned white, too. Most men, he told himself, were probably desperately afraid their first time under fire, but an officer especially must try not to show it. As the shells whistled overhead, he called out to his gun squad in a voice that he hoped sounded calm:

"Sounds like wild geese flying over—only a little noisier."

Sickly grins ran along the column. Well, that was good enough. What more could be expected of troops that were certainly no veterans. They looked like the artisans, shop-keepers, and farmers they were, marching to war in their working clothes. Only Andrews and a few of the other officers had managed to outfit themselves in the artillery's uniform of cockaded tricorne, blue coat with scarlet facings, and buff-colored breeches.

The horses of the gun teams plainly showed their terror at the British bombardment. They reared and plunged wildly. Drivers astride the lead animal of each pair in tandem kept the teams in control, though gunners had to grasp the bridles of the riderless rear horses to steady them. On rolled the six cannon. Andrews glanced proudly at the one of which he was in charge. It did not belong to the three rescued from the schoolhouse, having been added to them later. For a while that quartet was all the field artillery of the American army until other cannon were obtained from towns around Boston and from captured British ships. Today this still unnamed gun would represent "Hancock," "Adams," and "Mistress Lucy," which were being held in reserve in the rear.

Wheels rumbled, and the hill loomed closer. Captain Sam Trevett, commanding the platoon consisting of Andrews' gun and one other, barked a command:

"Close up. Walk out those horses faster."

A good officer, Sam Trevett, Andrews reflected. He inspired far more confidence than their superior, old Colonel Richard Gridley, although Gridley was a veteran of the siege that had stormed French Louisbourg in 1758. If only Henry Knox had been in command of the artillery! But he had been detailed as an engineer to build more of the fortifications ringing Boston. Knox, Andrews had heard, had recommended that the redoubt they were now approaching be constructed on Bunker Hill, a stronger position than Breed's.

Now they were under the brow of the hill and safe for the time from the shells screaming overhead. Trevett called out:

"Unlimber. Teams to the rear."

As the guns were uncoupled, and the horses wheeled the limbers and left the redoubt, he spoke quietly to his lieutenant. "That's the last we're likely to see of the teams, Andrews. I doubt if the drivers, civilians and no soldiers, will risk their lives and animals coming back for us. If we have to get out of here, be ready to manhandle the guns."

"Yes, sir."

"All right. Prepare for action. Hold on—wait! There are no embrasures in this confounded fort!"

The fort builders, completely ignorant of artillery, had raised an earthen wall without cutting any openings through which cannon could fire.

"How in creation do they expect us to do any shooting?" Trevett angrily demanded. "Hoist our guns up on the parapet beside that soldier there?"

As he spoke, the man, who had mounted to the top of the earthworks to watch the enemy, was struck squarely by a cannonball. His mangled body toppled back into the redoubt.

"Not healthy up there," Trevett said calmly. "Stand back, you men," he called to musketeers behind the defenses, then gave rapid orders to his platoon. His artillerymen rolled the guns up close to the earthen wall, fired and blasted gaps through it, making their own embrasures.

The cannon, loaded again, peered down the slope, and none too soon.

"The Redcoats! They're coming!" The exultant shout, picked up, ran along the length of the intrenchments.

Over the barrel of his gun Andrews stared down at the Charles River. Oars, dipping and flashing, drove barge after barge, crammed with grenadiers and light infantry from the Boston garrison. There must be between 2,000 and 3,000 of them. Sunlight glinted on the brass of cannon in the bows of several of the heavily laden craft. The Royal Artillery, its guns far outnumbering the Americans', was on its way into action.

With awed admiration Andrews watched the scarlet-clad companies disembark, form ranks, march forward. On they came, colors fluttering, officers out in front with drawn swords, bayoneted muskets so evenly sloped they seemed a single-angled surface. Faintly at first, then more loudly, rose the shrilling of the fifes and the rhythmic rattling of the drums. Ah, the beautiful precision, the martial splendor of it! Only the King's elite regiments of the Line could dress ranks like that, marching uphill to an assault.

The redoubled fury of the cannonade from the British frigates covering the advance jerked Andrews out of his trance. He heard Colonel Prescott shouting above the din to Trevett to take his two guns and follow Captain Knowlton's Connecticut troops out of the redoubt and down to the left toward the Mystic River. British battalions moving in that direction would soon turn the American left if they were not halted. Cannoneers sprang to the trails, to the dragropes and wheels.

Bluff old General Putnam met them, yelling an order. "Man the rail fence. The enemy's flanking us fast!"

Connecticut troops and Stark's New Hampshire volunteers ran to obey "Old Put," distributing themselves along the fence which extended down to the shore, though its upper end left an ominous, 200 yard gap between it and the redoubt. They strengthened the fence with stones and packed in new-mown hay—a flimsy defense but somehow a Yankee felt better if his shins at least were under cover. Muskets and fowling pieces poked over the top rail, their muzzles lowered, fixing on the oncoming grenadiers like rigidly pointed fingers.

"Hold your fire. Wait for the order." Officers passed the word along the line.

Trevett called out to his platoon, "That means us, too. Bombardiers, keep those matches away from the vents." Anxiously and impatiently he ground a heel into the soil, for downhill the British infantry had halted to let their artillery open. Now was the time for American counter-battery fire. But there was sudden confusion among the gun crews of the six-pounders down there. Obviously they were in some sort of trouble with their ammunition.

"Captain!" Andrews cried jubilantly. "They can't load. Looks like some fool filled their side-boxes with twelve-pound balls."

Trevett laughed, and answered, "You're right. They can't ram those balls into the muzzles. But we'll hear from them later at closer range. They'll load with grapeshot now."

Fire from the naval vessels had ceased, and the British came on in silence except for the beat of drums and the music of fifes. Andrews, watching tensely, was gripped by a strange sense of unreality. This was like a parade, a military pageant, with no resemblance to the grim and deadly business of war as he had read of it. Was this to be another Fontenoy, where British and French battalions had confronted each other without a shot until the former's commander politely requested, "Gentlemen of France, fire first"?

Two hundred yards. The fifes were loud now, and Andrews caught the tune, "The Three Cheers," though human throats uttered none. Under the burning afternoon sun the scarlet tunics of the grenadiers loomed like an advancing wall of flame.

One hundred yards. American marksmen could not miss at that range. Would the order to fire never be given? A minute or two and those shining British bayonets would sweep in, thrusting.

A mighty bellow burst from "Old Put" at last. "Powder's scarce. Fire low. Aim at their waistbands. Wait till you see the whites of their eyes. Aim at those handsome coats. Pick off the officers. *Fire!*"

Andrews' ears rang with the deafening crash of the volley, its echoes redoubled by the fire from the fort up the hill to his right. He saw the ball from his cannon blast a lane through the close-packed array. It was like the blade of a plow, cutting a long, bloody furrow. Far more appalling was the effect of the musketry—as if a gigantic scythe had mown down a field of poppies. In the arc of its swath lay bodies, still or feebly struggling. Almost all the officers in the forefront were down. The leading companies of grenadiers and light infantry had dropped in serried rows, their beautiful alignment scarcely disturbed. It was the ranks of their support that were broken, driven reeling back down the hill in wild disorder. Trevett's guns scourged them, booming above triumphant cheers.

"With grapeshot, charge pieces," Trevett ordered. "They'll be back."

Musket men along the fence stared back in disbelief, but Andrews and Sergeant Sampson kept their cannoneers at their task. No man who knew the British Army and its traditions could doubt it would attack again in spite of its bloody repulse. Only fifteen minutes had passed when upward marched the re-formed ranks again, up against fence and fort, never halting to fire, though the Royal Artillery was in action at last, and shells were bursting over the defenses. The relentless advance of those steady phalanxes, the gleam of their bayonets, the very sight of scarlet coats which had won their terrible name on a hundred battlefields—those had driven in the wedge of many a victory.

Along the American lines the word was passed once more. "Wait! Hold your fire." Officers knocked up the barrels of too-eager muskets.

Now the enemy was close again, and this time Andrews recognized the troops marching toward him. White tassels on tall bearskin caps, royal blue facings on scarlet tunics—a flank company of the Royal Welch Fusiliers. That debonair young officer in front was David Thorpe and he was directly under the muzzle of Andrew's gun.

Pity and horror swelled in the American's throat. Blasting a man he had called his friend into eternity was intolerable. An order to shift the trail of his piece, an order he knew he had no right to utter, was on his lips. Before he could speak, muskets near him cracked, and Thorpe crumpled to the ground. Grape from the roaring cannon swept above his body.

Blinding, choking smoke swirled up to reveal the same ghastly slaughter, windrows of British dead whose white breeches gave the field the look of a fold of sleeping sheep. Yonder down the hill some of the survivors were trying to get into their boats. Officers beat them back with the flats of their swords.

Trevett wiped his streaming brow and sighed. "They'll try again," he foretold. "And our powder's nearly gone."

It was true of all the defenders. Last grains were being tilted from many a powder horn. Few soldiers had bayonets to meet a British charge.

An artillery officer, breathing hard, hurried down from the fort and confronted Trevett. "Move your guns back to Charlestown, Captain," he said.

Trevett frowned and asked, "Whose orders?"

"Colonel Gridley's, I presume. You must be nearly out of powder as we are in the fort."

"Still in position up there, aren't you?"

"Yes, but it's not our fault. We tried to withdraw and replenish our ammuntion. 'Old Put' drove us back at the point of his pistol. It's crazy to stay on. You'll lose your guns as we will ours."

Sam Trevett stared at him boldly. "I'm staying here," he snapped. "Suppose you get back where you belong and do your duty." The officer, his face crimson, walked hastily away. Turning, Trevett met his lieutenant's eyes.

"It's an honor to serve under you, sir," Kent Andrews said quietly.

"Thanks. We'll give 'em a few more rounds."

The tall, commanding figure of General Howe was seen leading the third assault. Still unwavering but wearily, more slowly, the remnants of his regiments followed. The spectacle drew a gasp of admiration from Andrews. Those Redcoats could not know the Americans' powder was almost gone. They must believe they were marching to certain death. This time the main column was directed toward the fort, and only a small force threatened the river flank. Its puzzled defenders were not long left in ignorance of the British strategy. In through that fatal upper gap between fence and redoubt plunged the crashing shells of the Royal Artillery.

American musketeers and gunners were dropping fast. Enfiladed, the position was hopeless. Every man in it would soon be killed or cut off and captured. Andrews through the tumult somehow caught Trevett's order. He found himself tugging at his gun's dragrope along with the captain and Bombardier Brooks, two more cannoneers straining at the wheels. Big Sergeant Sampson was holding up the trail alone. There were only enough of them to save one of the guns—Andrews'. Heaving away, they hauled the piece toward the redoubt.

They were staggering and panting when they reached the hilltop. But there was no refuge for them in the fort nor any need of them there. The last volleys of its defenders had dwindled to scattered shots. British grenadiers were on the parapets, bayonets stabbing down. The artillerymen, skirting the fort, joined its surviving defenders streaming to the rear. Down the hill to the south, Charlestown was in flames; British warships had bombarded it to dislodge American sharpshooters. Twice Trevett halted his gun and fired its last two rounds to cover the retreat. Then they rolled past Bunker Hill, behind Breed's and across Charlestown Neck to safety.

One gun saved out of six! Andrews leaned, exhausted and dispirited, on its smoke-grimed carriage. Dogged British valor had won the day. If only our powder had held out, he thought, we might have— Yet that was vain speculation. "Ifs" and "might-have-beens"— those were invisible legends on drooping banners borne by every vanquished army in history from a stricken field. But we stood up to them, he told himself, and twice we smashed them back.

"Fight the good fight. Quit yourselves like men." That

ringing line from the Bible ran through Andrews' mind. It was Saint Paul, he remembered, who had spoken those gallant words.

Well, Andrews thought, we lived up to those words even if we had to give up the hill. And we save this gun of mine.

He patted its still-hot barrel. "Time you had a name," he said. What should it be? Hadn't Henry Knox mentioned a battery of olden days named for the Twelve Apostles? Let this gun be named for one who joined them—for Saint Paul, a man as valiant as his speech.

The four guns. Namesakes of two bold statesmen, a brave lady, and a great saint. Though a battle had been lost, they must help win a war.

Chapter V

General Washington's Mission

THE fight on Breed's Hill, which would come to be called the Battle of Bunker Hill, was defeat but far from disaster. According to trustworthy reports trickling out of Boston, British casualties had exceeded one thousand, while the raw American militia, who had twice repulsed Regulars, had lost less than four hundred and fifty in killed and wounded.

Gaps in the ranks were slowly being filled, and drillmasters were busy. A new general arrived to take command of the Army—George Washington of Virginia—a good soldier with service in the Indian wars, Andrews was told. But what more could General Washington do than tighten the cordon around Boston? He could not compel the town to surrender without more and heavier guns.

Some were being made in Philadelphia, and Paul Revere was striving to establish a foundry in Massachusetts and turn from casting bells to cannon. But it would be many months before the light guns in the forts Knox had built to ring in Boston could be replaced by more powerful ordnance. Andrews knew that howitzers and mortars would be needed to blast the British out.

As the siege dragged on through summer into fall, Andrews rode often to the American outer lines. Perhaps some of the townsmen who slipped out of Boston from time to time to join the Rebels would bring him word of his mother and Constancy Waite. Surely no harm would come to them, but they must be on short rations like everyone in the beleagured town, including British troops and Tory citizens. Patriots would be faring the worst, and Andrews was worried.

At last he saw a familiar figure being halted by the pickets. It was the schoolmaster, Abraham Holbrook. As soon as he was examined and passed, he hastened up to his friend.

"All's well with your mother, Kent," he reported. "She's a bit hungry like the rest of us, but endures bravely. She sent her love. She heard about your conduct in the battle and she's proud of you.

"There's some bad news, too," the schoolmaster went on, and Andrews' mouth tightened. "The British and Tories looted Henry Knox's book shop. His brother William he'd left in charge couldn't stop them. The place was gutted. All those fine books were stolen. The Lobsters were furious Henry wouldn't take a commission in their army."

Andrews broke in to ask, "By the way have you chanced to see Constancy Waite?"

Holbrook grinned at the casual manner of the question.

"Indeed I have," he said. "Our fair messenger of warning at the schoolhouse that night. As good to look upon as ever." Then, annoyingly, he shifted the subject.

"You people certainly gave it to the King's men on the hill that day!" he declared jubilantly. "Their hospitals are still jammed with wounded. They've overflowed into homes. I saw that Welch Fusilier officer you knew. Thorpe, wasn't that his name? He was pretty badly hit."

"I know. I saw him fall."

"Did you? That was hard—facing a man, who used to be your friend, on a battlefield. Well, he's going to recover."

"I can't help being glad he will, Abraham."

"You're the kind that would be, Kent. His recovery will be due to the family taking care of him. They're Americans, not Tories, which is to the credit of their Christian charity toward an enemy. Ah, yes. That was where I saw Constancy. Ensign Thorpe is being cared for in the Waites' home. Constancy's a wonderful nurse and a devoted one. Show me the way to Headquarters, will you? I have a report to make."

Andrews hoped his expression had not betrayed his jealousy. All too well he could picture Constancy bending over her wounded charge, her hands smoothing his brow. A woman's heart going out to a helpless man—even more to a man of proven valor, and a handsome one, enemy or not. His thoughts made him wince. There was more reason than ever now for the American army to take Boston and be quick about it.

A company swung marching toward them. Its ranks were ragged, its firearms of crazy variety, and few men boasted a complete uniform, but there was spirit in these recruits. They were roaring out "Yankee Doodle," which the Americans had taken from the British for their own, making up new verses.

> Father and I went down to camp,
>   Along with Cap'n Gooding,
> And there we see the men and boys
>   As thick as hasty pudding.
> Yankee Doodle, keep it up,
>   Yankee Doodle, dandy,
> Mind the music and the step,
>   And with the girls be handy.

Andrews bit his lip. How that last line rankled now! With his girl, it was another man who was handy.

Holbrook had turned to watch the company. "Good lads," he said. They'll do all right if they don't run out of powder as you did on the hill. Has the supply been replenished?"

"Somewhat, but it's still tarnal short," Andrews answered. "In the artillery we haven't enough to fire such guns as we have for more than a few hours in action."

At Headquarters in Cambridge, bustling and greatly changed now in November from its early days, Andrews heard his name called out by an aide.

"Been looking for you everywhere, Lieutenant Andrews. Report at once to Colonel Knox."

"*Colonel* Knox?"

"Right. General Washington appointed him. Knox is the new Chief of Artillery."

Chief of Artillery of the Continental Army at twenty-five! It was like some improbable happening in a book. Well, it was from a book that Knox had learned enough gunnery to impress Washington, and the Commander-in-Chief, from all one heard of him, was not easily impressed.

Andrews, his worries submerged, hastened to find and congratulate his commander.

Knox was already in uniform. Mistress Lucy had managed to find enough scarce blue cloth for her husband's bulk, and had cut and sewn a handsome coat and adorned its shoulders with glittering epaulettes. But the new-made Colonel, though he was obviously proud of his rank, could talk of nothing but General Washington, and Andrews had never heard him speak more earnestly and humbly.

"That first day I met the General—I showed him the fortifications at Roxbury—I knew I stood in the presence of a very great man," Knox avowed. "He's every inch the soldier, Kent. Sits his horse with back straight as a ramrod but with the ease of the fox hunter I'm told he is. His face and bearing seem austere. It rather chills you at first until you realize it's actually great dignity. I'd even call it majesty. That's a better name for it. Such majesty as I've never seen in portraits of kings. Certainly none of it appears on the pudgy features of that fat German who sits on the British throne, George the Third. I tell you, Kent, our General's a man to follow anywhere."

"We'll follow him, sir, with our guns."

"We'll do more. We'll bring him the guns he needs here."

Andrews stared at his chief. "Where in the world will we get them?" he asked.

"From Fort Ticonderoga. Guns are there, heavy ones, guns to spare. They've been in American hands since Ethan Allen and Benedict Arnold captured the fort last May. I suggested an expedition to bring the guns here from Fort Ti, and General Washington is going to let me make it."

Fort Ticonderoga in northern New York, somewhere

between Lake Champlain and Lake George, wasn't it? That was many miles away. Andrews looked his doubt and remarked, "But winter's coming on, sir."

"That's our answer. Snow for ox sleds. Ice bridging the rivers."

Andrews eagerly asked, "When will the expedition start, sir?"

"Soon now. Without a word about the mission, muster at once the best men from our old platoon of the Grenadier Corps. Can you lay hands on them?"

"Most of them, sir. A few were Tories who stayed in Boston. Some were killed on the hill. I'll have the rest standing by. We'll be ready."

Knox bent a stern look on him. "You seem to assume you're going, Lieutenant Andrews. You must be aware how badly good drillmasters are needed here in camp. General Washington would hardly approve my taking all my experienced men along."

The big man bellowed with laughter at the look of utter dismay on his subordinate's face. Those guns at Fort Ti would have to be heavy ones to roar louder than Henry Knox when he let his great voice go.

"All right, Kent," he said when his laughter had subsided. "Be ready."

General Washington had warned that the mission must be kept a profound secret. If any word of it leaked out through spies, surely the British would make every effort to cut off the guns before they could reach the American lines around Boston.

Two groups took horse and quietly slipped out of camp. Henry Knox and his younger brother William rode west through central New York to arrange with General Schuyler, commanding there, for relays of horses, oxen, and sleds to transport the guns. A little later Lieutenant Kent Andrews mustered the second party, its core made up of his old comrades of the artillery train: Sergeant Sampson, Bombardier Brooks, and others. Choosing the most direct route northwest to Fort Ticonderoga, they pressed forward through the sharpening cold of late fall on their high adventure.

CHAPTER VI

Fort Ti and "The Old Sow"

OVER the party of approaching horsemen loomed the ramparts of Fort Ticonderoga, rising massive and formidable on the neck of land between Lakes George and Champlain. Kent Andrews, his platoon of picked artillerymen at his back, stared with awe at the stone bastions standing athwart the path of armies marching from Canada. How gravely the loss of this splendid stronghold must have irked the British high command! The Yankees of Allen and Arnold had captured it so easily in that surprise night attack last May.

Visible now were the muzzles of many cannon, frowning down from their embrasures. Those guns, if they could be brought back over the weary way the artillerymen had come, might prove to be iron keys to unlock the gates of Boston.

51

Andrews' horse and the others, sensing feed and stables
ahead, quickened their pace. As the cavalcade climbed the
causeway, sentries challenged, then passed the artillerymen in. The tired riders dismounted in the Place d'Armes,
its name retained from the days when Fort Ti was France's
Fort Carillon. Andrews glanced curiously toward a house
which must have been the quarters of the British com-
mandant when Ethan Allen at the head of his Green
Mountain men burst in and demanded surrender "in the
name of the Great Jehovah and the Continental Congress."
Or had the lusty Vermonter roared at the British captain,
as some said, "Come out, you damned old rat!"? That,
from all Andrews had heard of Ethan Allen, sounded more
like him.

Henry Knox came striding out of the house to welcome
them. By rides averaging forty miles a day, the Colonel, in
spite of his long detour, had reached Fort Ti ahead of his
artillerymen. Though he had only recently arrived, he
looked fresh as a daisy and seemed not to have lost a
pound of his bulk.

"Glad you're here, men," he called out. "Stable and feed
your horses and get something to eat yourselves. Then
report back. No time to lose. I want to get our guns moving."

In high spirits, Knox showed them some sixty cannon
he had chosen to take to the siege of Boston, cannon that
could be spared out of the hundred or more in the fort
and by no means leave it defenseless. His artillerymen already were familiar with the types of guns—Knox had
selected calibres from long twenty-four-pounders down
to sixes, both brass and iron—but it was necessary for him
to identify the various other sorts, designed for use in
sieges. Those, he explained, were howitzers whose angle

of fire, higher than a gun's, let them lob shells over hills or walls to burst in the midst of enemy sheltered behind them. Here were mortars, less mobile than howitzers because they were not mounted on carriages but fixed on their own platforms or "beds" and transported on sturdy four-wheeled wagons called block carriages or dragged on stoneboats, used by farmers to haul rocks from fields. The mortars, which ranged from small coehorns, named after the Dutch baron who invented them, to three monstrous ones with bore diameters of thirteen inches, fired heavier projectiles than howitzers at far more steeply curved arcs of flight.

For use in lifting the gun barrels on or off their carriages, many of them had been cast with handles above the trunnions called dolphins because they were shaped like the fish whose namesake they were.

Eph Brooks bent to slap the short tube of the largest of the three big mortars. He grinned and grunted, *"Oink."* The mortar, squat and ponderous, resembled a fat black pig.

"Colonel," the gunner said, "Lieutenant Andrews told us all guns ought to be named. I've got a name for this one. Not a highfalutin one, but I figure it fits."

"Let's have it, Brooks."

" 'The Old Sow,' sir."

Knox burst out with a loud guffaw. " 'The Old Sow' she is," he agreed, "and you can herd her to Boston, Brooks. Just get her aboard that stoneboat there and drag her down to the lake. If you need any help—"

"Don't call on me," Sergeant Sampson said and dug his elbow into the ribs of the discomfited bombardier.

So on the sixth day of December, 1775, they began their tremendous task of moving sixty tons of cannon by water and land, over hills and through valleys, 300 miles to the heights around Boston where General Washington awaited them.

With the garrison pitching in and lending willing hands, Knox's men removed the cannon from the ramparts of Fort Ti. Most of them were mounted on garrison carriages, like those of ships' guns, with small iron wheels to let them roll back in recoil after firing. Such carriages would not serve to transport them far—log sleds must be used. It was the huge mortars which sat, wheelless, on their trunnions, bolted onto ironbound oak beds, that proved formidable. They had to be heaved and hauled and levered onto block carriages or stoneboats. Gunner Brooks, mopping his brow, after a struggle with a squad on "The Old Sow," heard Colonel Knox's voice consoling him.

"Never mind, Brooks. Artillery's much lighter than it used to be. Two and a half centuries ago you might have had to help move the Great Mortar of Moscow. It had a bore of thirty-six inches and was eighteen feet long. I don't know how heavy it was, but you can get an idea from the fact that it fired a stone ball weighing a ton."

"Thanks for the thought, sir," Brooks answered, grinning. "I can't tell you how it rests me."

At last all the guns, along with a score of boxes and barrels containing lead and flints, were transported to the shores of Lake George and loaded on scows. Long sweeps, manned with backbreaking toil, drove the clumsy flat-bottomed boats over the blue waters. Each evening the crews pulled ashore, moored and made camp, warming themselves at big fires. Progress was smooth and steady till midway in the voyage when fair weather gave way to a sudden squall which tossed the heavy-laden craft about as if they were skiffs, dashing waves over the gunwales.

Alternately bailing and rowing, the desperate, seasick men strove to keep afloat. One scow was swamped and sunk but its crew was saved.

At last they beached the flotilla at Fort George at the farther end of the lake and counted themselves lucky. The season of winter storms had set in; had it come a little sooner and more severely, a water crossing might have been impossible.

Now fell the hoped-for snow, thick and heavy, snow that would pave a way through the roadless woods and over the steep hills. More stout sleds were built and ready for the drivers and their teams, expected at this lake-end rendezvous.

Brooks looked wearily at "The Old Sow," squatted on her sled, and spoke to Colonel Knox. "I hope, sir, there'll be plenty of critters to pull this little pet of mine. I'm worn out hauling her along. She don't lead well."

"There'll be enough," Knox assured him with a chuckle. "I'll give you eight spans of oxen if you need them. But I tell you again you're fortunate to be an artilleryman in 1775. Two hundred years ago some guns were so large it took sixty horses to draw them."

Brooks was still muttering about his mistake in not joining the infantry, with only a musket to carry, when drivers herded a long column of oxen and horses into camp. Spans were hitched in, teamsters shouted, and forty sleds, creaking under their freight—some 5,000 pounds of metal on each—glided forward smoothly on their runners.

Bitter, freezing weather, unremitting labor. Oxen and horses, hoofs balled with snow, slipped and went down. They had to be helped to struggle back on their feet, pushed back into the traces, put in draft again. The artillerymen were out of their saddles constantly to shove and pry sleds loose from stumps and boulders. Not a man of them but knew he had never worked so hard in his life, and hoped never to again. The cold bit through mittens and boots to numbed fingers and toes, through greatcoats to stiffened joints. But the milestones of their journey slowly fell behind them: Fort George, Fort Edward, then Saratoga where a thaw halted them, and they had to wait for more snow to fall.

As the going grew heavier, teams were increased to eighty yoke of oxen and horses. Leading spans, plunging into great snowdrifts, sank out of sight and had to be dug out. Steep hills forced the doubling of teams on each load, and every hard climb meant repeated relays. Sleds broke down under their burden of metal and had to be repaired or replaced. The train, lengthening out, was divided into companies, often many miles apart. Knox rode ahead, arranging for fresh animals, or back along the column, directing, encouraging, and urging on his weary men.

But most of all it was the people along the route that put heart into the exhausted expedition. They came from cabins and farmhouses or lined village streets to watch the train pass, and in their eyes was wonder and pride. Here were guns going to General Washington, guns on their way to win the fight for liberty. Nor were the countryfolk and townsmen content only to wave and cheer. Eager volunteers came forward to help, and offers of food and shelter never failed.

Knox, glowing at their welcome, turned in his saddle to call to Andrews. "Guess we cut no small figure with this train of ours. What counts, though, is that these Yorkers are our people. I haven't had that feeling as strongly since the Colonies rallied to stand together at Bunker Hill. We're Americans, Kent. We'll make a nation."

"A nation." Andrews echoed quietly. It was a word that filled a man's mind.

Knox spoke on, smiling. "We'll let these folks hear how our guns sound. They deserve a little testimony. Halt for the night just beyond this village. Have Brooks charge 'The Old Sow' lightly with powder, touch her off, and let her grunt for them."

Brooks was delighted to show off the big mortar. He made an occasion of it, drafting a local fifer and drummer to furnish music. While women and girls passed mugs of hot buttered rum and mulled cider to grateful artillerymen and drivers, Eph took station beside the mortar and made a speech.

"This is my little pet, 'The Old Sow,'" he said. "Name suits her looks, don't it? She's the most valuable gun in the whole American army." He pointed to a load of small coehorns on a nearby sled. "See there, friends. Since we left Fort Ti, 'The Old Sow's' littered."

The crowd howled with laughter, and Eph went on. "When we get to Boston, she's going to bring the Lobsterbacks' barracks tumbling about their ears. I'll show you how, if my assistant, Sergeant Sampson, will oblige. Powder, Sergeant."

Sampson glared at his impudent subordinate, but passed up a powder bag. Brooks dropped it in the mortar's maw and rammed in wadding with a flourish. Priming the vent, he lit a linstock match.

"Hold your ears, girls," he warned. "'The Old Sow' grunts plenty loud."

His match swept down, and the mortar spoke with a mighty bellow that reverberated against the hills. Women and children screamed, men yelled, the drummer beat a long roll, and the fifer struck up *Yankee Doodle*. The crowd joined in, singing. After the first rollicking chorus ended, Eph held up his hand for attention and launched, inspired, on a later stanza that fitted the occasion as if it had been written for it.

> And there we see a swampin' gun,
>   As big as a log of maple,
> Upon a deuced little cart,
>   A load for father's cattle.
> And every time they shoot it off,
>   It takes a horn of powder,
> And makes a noise like father's gun,
>   Only a nation louder.

"Well done, Brooks," Knox congratulated the master of ceremonies. "We'll do it again along the route. And you shall have the honor of firing the first round from 'The Old Sow' when she's trained on Boston."

But could the guns reach Boston before the British were reinforced and broke the siege? The march was cruelly slow, slower even than the plodding pace of the oxen, because of breakdowns and natural obstacles. Three times they faced crossings of the upper Hudson over a frozen surface that did not seem solid enough to bear the heavy loads. Knox ordered holes cut in the ice, and after the water bubbled through, freezing in another layer, they were able to cross safely. At Albany a thaw halted them for days. When Knox, wracked by impatience, risked the Hudson ice a fourth time, the last sled in the train broke through, and the cannon on it, a long eighteen, was "drowned." Citizens rallied to help a shivering crew grapple and raise the 2,000 pounds of metal from the bottom, and in honor of the rescuers the salvaged gun was christened "Albany."

On to Kinderhook, Claverack, Nobletown, and east into Massachusetts where at Westfield "The Old Sow" performed again for a highly impressed audience. At Springfield the New Yorkers turned over the guns to drivers of their sister Colony who met the train with strong, fresh teams, sorely needed since warmer weather had turned the roads into muddy bogs. But they were on the last lap now and they pressed on.

Fifty days after the expedition left Fort Ticonderoga, on January 24th in a year that would be forever memorable —1776—the advance section dragged wearily into Cambridge. Andrews rode forward in time to join his commander for their entry into the American camp amid tumultuous enthusiasm. High-ranking officers crowded about Knox, and their juniors around his lieutenant, congratulating them and demanding the story of their epic achievement.

A lane opened, and General Washington strode through, his face alight with a smile that was an accolade.

"Your Excellency," Knox said, saluting, "I present you with a noble train of artillery."

Andrews watched the General take Knox's lowered hand in a strong grasp and heard him ask that when all sections of the train arrived they be paraded so that he could thank them personally. This was a leader who commanded not only men's actions but their devotion and loyalty.

A flash of bright colors drew Andrews' eyes from General Washington's tall, soldierly figure. Above Headquarters fluttered a new flag with thirteen stripes of red and white. Those must represent the Colonies fighting for liberty. In the corner the crosses of Saint Andrew and Saint George on a blue background stood for the British union; after Americans had irrevocably cut all ties with the mother country, the union would be replaced by a circle of stars. Though Kent Andrews saw the banner for the first time, somehow it stirred him deeply. There flew the flag of the nation Knox had said Americans were making, a flag for a man to follow all his life.

After the excitement over the arrival of the cannon had subsided, Andrews walked quietly to the old artillery park. There were friends there he must see, friends he had not forgotten—the four guns. Somehow an artilleryman kept his affection for the first pieces he served. They were like your first pistol or your first horse. Henry Knox was right. A cannon, though it was only a metal tube on wheels, possessed a personality.

There they stood. "Hancock" and "Adams," "Mistress Lucy" and "Saint Paul." Their barrels shone from polishing. Andrews was glad to see they had been well maintained during his absence. As he passed from one three-pounder to another, he turned to find Sergeant Sampson and Bombardier Brooks behind him, smiling understandingly.

"Kind of reunion we're having, sir," Brooks said. "Our threes here look sort of small and light after those twenty-fours and mortars we sledded from Ti."

"Heavy enough," Sampson put in. "Remember lugging three of them out of the gun-house that night? And before we were done hauling 'Saint Paul' back from Breed's Hill he felt like he weighed a ton."

Brooks' eyes twinkled. "Sergeant," he said, "that should have taught you never to take a saint lightly."

The big non-com gave him a sour look, but Andrews added: "Yes, these guns of ours will carry their weight for us. We need the heavy stuff we brought from Ti to blast the British out of Boston. But when we meet the Redcoats again, close up in battle, we'll count on these old friends. And if Colonel Knox allows it—and I think he will—I hope my old platoon will man them with me."

Sampson and Brooks spoke together. "We will, sir."

Chapter VII

Artillery Duel

ON Cobble Hill Bombardier Brooks, smoldering match in hand, stood at the breech of "The Old Sow," her gaping muzzle upturned and trained on Boston. Other artillerymen along the line of earthworks waited as tensely around their pieces. Here on the hill and in other fortifications the guns from Fort Ti were ready. The hour for which they had been brought over so many miles of snow, ice, and mud would strike tonight, March 2nd. General Washington had chosen to open fire on the town with the sudden shock of a night bombardment.

Once again Andrews and Sampson, like other officers and sergeants, checked the laying of heavy mortars and eighteen-pounders, carefully aimed during the afternoon at enemy defenses and barracks. Targets were well within

62

range, and the guns could not miss. But the light of hooded lanterns in the trenches revealed grim and anxious faces. The families of many of the cannoneers lived in Boston, and all whose homes were in the line of fire were in grave danger. Still there was no escape from hard necessity—no other way to break the British grip on a vital port than to blast it loose. Andrews could only hope that his mother and Constancy Waite would take refuge in the farther part of town as soon as the cannonade began.

Men around the guns spoke only in whispers so there would be not a second's delay in hearing and obeying the order to fire. Now it came—a shout from a major. The eighteens boomed first, shattering the silence. In a rush the mortar crews bent to their task. Matrosses heaved heavy shells up to the muzzles, lowering them down bores against charges. Brooks touched his match to the priming charge in "The Old Sow's" vent. His crew leaped back, holding their ears. The big thirteen-incher bellowed mightily, its shell fuse blazing a crimson trail across the black sky. Yonder in Boston it burst with a lurid flash that illuminated the roof of a British regiment's barracks, erupting and disintegrating under its roaring impact. As cheering Americans continued to serve their guns, cannon in the enemy's forts furiously replied, but their balls fell short. Iron rained down on Boston until Knox ordered a cease fire to save powder.

There was to be no sleep for the British. A second and a heavier bombardment was scheduled for the following night.

Meanwhile the most highly prized artillery piece in the army was brought forward and added to the battery on Cobble Hill. It was a handsome, bronze thirteen-inch mortar, captured from a British brig by an American privateer. The Ticonderoga men jealously watched the new-comer being put in position.

"Pretty brass trinket you got there," Brooks jibed. "Takes a deal of polishing, I wager. Will it really shoot, or is it just for looks?"

The rival mortar's gunner made a derisive gesture to-ward "The Old Sow" and snapped back. "Lug that chunk of rusty iron all the way from Fort Ti, did you? Might as well take it back or sell it to an ironmonger now that 'Congress' is here."

" 'Congress'? That what you call it?"

"Sure. 'Old Put' hisself named it. The General filled its barrel up with rum for the christenin'. Trouble was him and some other officers drunk most of it 'fore us in the crew could more'n wet our whistles."

"Never mind. That's a good name—'Congress.' Lots of noise and no action."

"Say you so? Show you tonight."

The two big mortars flamed and banged almost together, when the order to fire was given that evening. Their crews eagerly watched the shells soar aloft in graceful arcs, curve down and explode in Boston. They sprang forward to swab, reload and fire again.

"Short both times, you lads with the iron popgun," yelled "Congress's" gunner. "You didn't hit nothin'. Told you we'd show you. Now watch the next shot. Load 'er up, boys."

Grinning matrosses crammed the maw of the bronze mortar with ladle after ladle of powder.

"Take care!" Brooks called. "That's a tarnal heavy charge. You'll bust her!"

"Pull in them codfish eyes of your'n and mind your own business!" the other gunner shouted.

As the shell was lowered in, he swept his match down to the vent. "Congress" spoke with a tremendous voice, hurling its shell far into the town. But when the smoke cleared, lantern light showed a long, disabling crack along the bronze barrel, the result of the overcharge.

Brooks could not resist a taunt. "Well, friends," he drawled, "looks like 'Congress' has adjourned."

The guns thundered on. Shells raked the town and started fires that sent columns of flame leaping up against the sky. Yet Boston held out. Its garrison quickly put out the fires, and the Royal Artillery was still in action.

Long-range bombardment, Andrews realized, would not be enough to pave the way for the town to be stormed. The guns must be shifted closer in. When orders came to redouble the rate of fire the following night, he guessed that the artillery must be masking some major move of General Washington's.

His guess was right. Under cover of darkness and the din of the cannonade, a brigade of American Infantry advanced and fortified Dorchester Heights. The British awoke next morning to stare in dismay at Rebel earthworks, strengthened by logs and bundles of faggots, on high ground which commanded Boston and the southern approaches to its harbor.

Attack and capture the Heights, or surrender—that was General Howe's only choice. Once guns were emplaced there, as they soon would be, they could blow his troops out of Boston and sink his fleet. Hastily battalions were mustered and barges massed at the wharves to ferry them across the channel for an assault early next morning. At all costs, the Heights must be carried.

Watching Americans spotted the concentration of boats and troops and were warned. Clearly the Redcoats meant to make another Breed's Hill of the Heights and they were hard to stop. Every man who had been on the hill that day well remembered those three charges. Now was the time for light guns firing grapeshot and canister to break the ranks that would sweep up the slopes to take the heavy artillery on the Heights.

Kent Andrews and his men were ordered to turn over "The Old Sow" to another crew and man their own guns. With other light batteries they took position in hastily dug intrenchments down the slope. They must hold the line until the big cannon could be emplaced above them on the crest.

Andrews checked the field of fire of the four guns. "We've enough powder this time," he told his men. "The sentry on duty will rouse the battery one hour before dawn. They'll attack at first light. We've got to stop 'em or lose our guns. Turn in now."

But that night a gale, of almost hurricane force, descended with torrential rain. Drenched artillerymen crouched miserably beneath the scant shelter of the gun carriages.

Bombardier Brooks called out from under the barrel of Number Four: "The Bible says Saint Paul got shipwrecked once. He couldn't have been wetter than me and his namesake here."

"Never mind, Brooks," Andrews answered. "Think of what this weather is doing to the enemy."

In fact, it was ruinous. There was no assault at dawn. All day and through the following night the storm raged. It wrenched the British barges from their moorings and drove troops ready to fill them back to their barracks. Before the weather cleared, the Americans managed to strengthen their defenses on Dorchester Heights and to emplace all the big guns. Black muzzles glared down from the embrasures. Once they opened fire, Boston was doomed.

General Howe, now in command, realized that he could hold the town no longer. He issued orders for his army, and all Tories who wished to leave, to board the fleet for evacuation to Halifax. Then he let word filter out through the lines, knowing that Washington would hold the fire of his artillery and spare Boston and the patriots remaining within its gates.

On the last day of turmoil and confusion Ensign David Thorpe, his wounds healed, came to bid Constancy Waite farewell.

"This may be my last chance to see you," he said sadly. "This must be good-by." He fingered his tall Fusilier's cap distractedly. "Once more an enemy officer thanks you for nursing him back to life."

"I just can't think of you as an enemy, David," the girl instantly protested. "You serve your King and his cause. Our soldiers serve our cause. Your army and ours are fighting for what each believes is right. Oh, if our differences could only have been settled without all this bloodshed! Aren't we the same people! My family came from Devon, not far from your Wales. Why must we—"

"Constancy!" Hope was bright on David Thorpe's handsome face. He took the girl's hands in his and looked deep into her blue eyes. "Listen. I've wondered often whether you took me into your home and nursed me only out of kindness and charity?"

"For any wounded man I would have done all I could,"

she answered, "but it made me especially happy to take care of a friend."

Thorpe's eyes clouded at the last word. A friend—she regarded him as no more. Perhaps it might be different after the war was won, but courtship was futile now.

"I understand," he said sadly. "It's Kent Andrews then."

"No. No, it isn't Kent. He's a dear friend—as you are. It's more than any person. This war has raised a barrier between us, between Britain and America. Can't you see, David, that your King forfeited his right to rule us when he used force to compel our obedience—to take our freedom from us?"

Thorpe bowed his head. Without another word he hurried from the house.

British frigates and transports were being crammed to the bulwarks. Nine thousand troops marched aboard with all the military equipment for which space could be found; perforce great quantities were left behind for hasty, partial destruction by rear-guard parties. Twelve hundred Tories—among them Lucy Knox's parents, the Fluckers— abandoned, heartsick, the homes they would never see again, piled their most precious possessions on decks and sought shelter. In the stormy voyage before them, as many as thirty-seven would be packed together in a single cabin.

Army discipline in Boston broke under the strain of the last chaotic hours before sailing, and officers, overwhelmed by duties, could not restrain all the pillaging bands of soldiers and seamen. But the most outrageous plundering was committed under the sanction of General Howe who, in an unguarded moment, authorized Crean Brush, an Irish-born Tory official, to confiscate all the linen and woolens in town and put them aboard the ships of the fleet.

Brush, rapacious and ruthless, gathered a gang of roughs and led it in a series of violent raids. They battered down doors of shops, gutted them and sent carts heaped high with goods to be loaded aboard a waiting brigantine. Soon her hold was crammed with a cargo of stolen property worth a great sum of money. Still Brush and his looters were not content. They began breaking into dwelling houses.

A few hours before sailing time they pushed their way into the Waites' home. While Constancy and her mother stood by helplessly, the scoundrels ripped quilts, blankets, and linen from beds and snatched clothing from chests and closets. Neither Mistress Waite's tears nor her daughter's frantic protests moved them. As soon as the robbers left with their spoils, Constancy sent a neighbor boy running to the barracks of the Royal Welch Fusiliers. Far sooner than she dared expect, the lad came panting back with an official-looking paper. Constancy scanned it with satisfaction. There was no time to spare. Without delaying to call her mother and show her the order, she hastened to the water front.

Crean Brush scowled down from the gangway of the brigantine at the pretty girl who came hurrying along the dock.

"Clear out of here, you!" he shouted. "I've no time for wenches now. What do you want?"

"The property you stole from my home," Constancy boldly declared.

"Do you now?" Brush snarled. "There's nothing stolen here. Only goods requisitioned from Rebels by General Howe's orders. Be off with you. You'll get none of it."

The girl thrust the paper toward him. "This will change your mind. You'd best read it or take the consequences."

A signature caught the Tory's eye. He grabbed the sheet from her hand and scanned it, mumbling aloud. "'On the representation of Ensign Thorpe, Royal Welch Fusiliers, it is determined that certain property, confiscated from a citizen, shall be returned to her. . . . His recovery from battle wounds due to her. . . . Restore said property to bearer at once. . . . By command of General Howe."

Brush looked up with an ugly smirk. "So that's how it stands. Yourself has influence, Mistress, I see. You're a Loyalist then?"

"All that concerns you is that I'm a victim of thieves."

The fellow shrugged indifferently. "Have it as you like. Come aboard then and take your stuff—if you can find it. The goods are below in the hold."

Tossing her yellow curls, Constancy hastened up the gangplank and descended a ladder through the main hatchway. Scarcely had she disappeared when a naval officer hailed the brigantine from a cutter that sped up alongside.

"Ahoy there! Join the convoy immediately or the fleet will not wait for you."

The brigantine's skipper answered with a surly "Aye," but turned to Brush before issuing orders. "That girl's still below," he reminded him.

A crafty look spread over the Tory's wizened face. The girl was probably the sweetheart of that Fusilier who had interceded for her, evidently an officer with weight at headquarters. No doubt he'd be delighted to see her again if she turned up in Halifax. Like as not she'd be just as pleased once she got over her fright at being carried off on a voyage "by mistake."

Brush cracked his knuckles gleefully. It took a smart

man to turn any old chance that cropped up to his advantage. He gave the skipper an answer.

"The girl's a passenger, Captain. Friend of a high-placed officer. She's skipped out from her Rebel family to join him in Halifax. Cast off and make sail."

As the crew hauled in the moorings, Brush slid the cover over the hatch. Only he heard the muffled screams that soared up from the blackness of the hold.

While the last of Howe's rear guard shoved off in small boats to board warships for the retreat to Canada, a thousand men under General Israel Putnam marched into rejoicing Boston. After them in happy homecoming thronged a concourse of citizens who had escaped from the town during the siege. They moved through streets packed by people who had been forced to endure those long, bitter months, people who cheered and laughed and cried, tears coursing down wan, hunger-pinched cheeks.

Kent Andrews, marching with the vanguard by Colonel Knox's special permission, could barely keep from breaking ranks and running ahead. Now at last he was home. There was his mother, holding out her arms to him. A captain called out, "Dismissed, Lieutenant Andrews. We'll manage without you." As he embraced his weeping mother, he saw Mistress Waite standing, pale and distraught, by her side. All his life he would remember the dreadful shock of the news they poured out. Constancy was missing. Perhaps she had gone to the docks yesterday morning to recover stolen goods from a ship. Friends were still scouring the town, but there was no trace of her. She must have been carried off by that scoundrel of a Tory, Crean Brush.

Andrews' furious, wildly anxious search led him to the

wharf where the brigantine had been moored. He found a fisherman's wife, who had watched the vessel load. Yes, she'd seen a girl go aboard, a girl with yellow curls. One of the Britishers' fancy women, she'd thought, for she'd gone below at once and never come back on deck when a Tory with an ugly Irish phiz on him ordered the ship to sail.

Henry Knox, on hearing his lieutenant's desperate appeal, went directly to General Washington. By the earliest and speediest means available a messenger under a flag of truce would be sent to Halifax with a demand for Constancy's release, the General promised. Surely General Howe, a soldier and a gentleman, would honor it—would do all in his power to see to it that the girl Brush must have kidnapped was returned unharmed. Nothing more could be done, and meanwhile weeks, even months, must pass.

Chapter VIII

March to Battle

INFANTRY boots, hoofs of teams, and wheels of rumbling gun carriages churned the dust of roads, dried by the summer sun. A gray film clogged throats and nostrils and covered the varicolored uniforms of foot regiments and the blue-with-scarlet-facings of Knox's artillery. General Washington's army, forcing the pace, pressed on from captured Boston toward New York.

"Close up!" Kent Andrews shouted gruffly to his battery. "Pick up your feet and quit straggling. Walk your horses out, you drivers. Keep your interval."

It was hard to prevent a column from stringing out on a long march. Officers and sergeants could not let their men drop back to avoid eating so much dust of the lot ahead, for a gap of yards soon lengthened into a quarter mile. Then it must be double time and trot to catch up.

"Close up!" Andrews barked again. Orders called for forced marches, and there was no time to lose. A British fleet and army might even now be sailing down from Halifax to redeem the loss of Boston by taking the equally vital port of New York.

In spite of urgency, hot and weary troops had begun to lag when a squad, then a company, started to sing. Andrews lifted his head to listen to the tune that was quickening steps of wilting marchers all along the column. It was William Billings' battle hymn, *Chester*.

> Let Tyrants shake their iron rod,
> And Slav'ry clank her galling chains.
> We fear them not . . .

Puritan fervor was still strong in these countrymen of his, Andrews thought. This song, which a leather tanner, turned musician, had composed in the glow of patriotism, stirred men's hearts. Voices in every rank caught up the words.

> We fear them not: we trust in God.
> New England's God forever reigns.

Ephraim Brooks, the green worsted knot of a corporal on his right shoulder now, called over, grinning, to his lieutenant:

"Guess we're going to share New England's God with the Yorkers and maybe even with the Pennsylvania Dutch."

Andrews nodded, smiling back. Brooks was right. It was one country Americans were fighting for now, and if they did not stand together, the cause was lost. As soldiers from other Colonies had come to defend Breed's Hill and storm Boston, so must Massachusetts rally to help save New York. He remembered another refrain that declared it: that of John Dickinson's *Liberty Song*—"By uniting we stand, by dividing we fall."

Singing carried the column on until it was halted for the night. Exhausted men flung themselves down under bushes and trees, but officers and non-coms routed them out, grumbling. No one could rest before sentries were posted and camp fatigue done.

A matross in Andrews' platoon, one of the loudest of the grumblers, complained bitterly as he worked.

"Got a slave-driver for a lieutenant, we have. It's dead-beat we are, but he makes us take off wheels and grease axles. Then it's check ammunition in the chests and side-boxes. Next it's line guns, limbers, and carts up like they was on dress parade in what he calls a park. After that we gotta cover 'em with tarpaulins so's they don't ketch cold."

The matross paused for breath, then growled on. "After that we're through 'cept for washing ourselves and brushing off our uniforms. Maybe then a man can eat and sleep if 'tain't his turn for guard or. . . ."

The complainer broke off to find Sergeant Sampson glowering down on him. "Connors," the Sergeant snapped, "its not your turn for guard but you can take an extra tour to learn to keep your trap shut. While you're walking your post, get it through your thick head that this is the best battery in the regiment 'cause Lieutenant Andrews makes it that way."

But there were furrows in the Sergeant's brow when he dropped back. Most of the details the matross had griped about were part of good march discipline and proper maintenance; but Andrews was driving the men hard, though no harder than he drove himself. He must be fretting about that girl of his. Even good officers got overfussy, often without realizing it, when some personal worry was gnawing at them.

Certainly Constancy Waite's disappearance had filled Andrews with desperate anxiety. Besides his fears for her safety he was torn with suspicion that David Thorpe might have had something to do with her sudden departure from Boston. Of course, the Fusilier must have fallen in love with her while she was nursing him back to health. Perhaps he had persuaded her to join him in Halifax and marry him there, and she had gone willingly.

Andrews sighed heavily and went off to inspect the guard. There was nothing he could do but wait for news, which might not come for months. Meanwhile he must find respite in action, in battles that surely lay ahead.

At last the army reached the Connecticut shore. Footsore men in vast relief loaded equipment, guns, and teams into barges and boats and were ferried down Long Island Sound. Soon they saw the houses of New York town looming beyond the battery which guarded the approaches to Manhattan Island. When Andrews and his men landed, they recognized some of the cannon in the fort as Ticonderoga guns. Colonel Knox, who had brought them down by ship while the seas were still clear of British frigates, came forward to welcome his regiment. He introduced his officers to a young captain of New York artillery, Alexander Hamilton, to whom Andrews took an immediate liking.

Washington's troops had arrived none too soon, for by the end of June sails of the vanguard of the British fleet were sighted. Towering ships of the line and frigates an-

chored off Sandy Hook, to be followed by crammed transports. Under cover of the fleet's guns, 20,000 red-coated
Regulars and blue-clad Hessians, hired out by their German princes to fight for King George, landed on Staten
and Long Islands. But no challenge was yet offered American troops farther south on Long Island or to the garrison
on Manhattan.

Meanwhile stirring news reached New York from Philadelphia—that on July 4th Congress had declared the Colonies to be free and independent States. The town went
wild with joy, its streets thronged by cheering citizens,
all the church bells pealing. Bonfires blazed up, kindled
by royal coats-of-arms and other symbols of British do-
minion, now cast off. Shouting Sons of Liberty and soldiers
hauled down the leaden statue of George III in Bowling
Green, to be melted into bullets and fired at His Majesty's
soldiers. Only Knox's cannon were silent during those
jubilant hours. Powder was too precious for salutes; it must
be saved for the enemy.

Andrews paraded with his battery in the formation of
troops ordered by General Washington, and listened to
the reading of the great Declaration. "When in the course
of human events . . ." Those majestic words held them
all spellbound through to the exalting end, when the
Signers boldly and resolutely dedicated their country and
themselves to the cause of freedom: "With a firm reliance
on the protection of Divine Providence, we mutually
pledge to each other our lives, our fortunes, and our sacred
honor."

The excitement swept on through that night with cele-
brations in homes and taverns. Corporal Brooks and Connors found jobs as extra tapsters at a banquet given at
Fraunces' Tavern. Next morning the two were so eager to

tell their lieutenant about that festive occasion that he could not refuse to listen.

"Lieutenant, you ought to have been there!" Brooks cried. "You sure missed something."

"Never et such vittles," Connors declared. "Made up for months of army rations. Plenty and to spare for the serv-ingmen. Black Sam Fraunces sets a grand table. Sides of beef, haunches of mutton, hog meat, turkey. Pickled and fried oysters, fit to send on to the West Indies. Cakes and sillabubs."

"Nothing to drink, I suppose," Andrews put in with a smile.

"They kept us tapsters on the run," Brooks admitted. "Madeira, port, porter, cider, spruce beer, sangaree, punch, and bitters—and I forget what else. No wonder Connors and I made a month's pay trundling tired gentlemen home in wheelbarrows afterwards."

"Sure and they had to drink all them toasts, didn't they?" Connors demanded. "Thirty-one of 'em there was, no less. Tell the Lieutenant some of 'em, Corp."

Brooks obliged. "Sir," he said, "they toasted Freedom, Congress, and the American army and navy."

"Don't forget that one I drank," Connors reminded him.

"A gentleman lifted his glass," Brooks related gleefully, "and proposed, 'May the generous sons of St. Patrick expel all the venomous reptiles of Britain.' Our hired tapster here cheered and stepped up and drank that one with the quality. Being Irish was all that saved him from getting tossed out on his ear.

"Oh, yes, there was another humdinger of a toast: 'The daughters of America—in the arms of their brave defend-ers only.'"

Brooks suddenly clapped his hand over his mouth and

turned crimson. What a thing to blurt out to Lieutenant Andrews after what had happened to his girl! The gunner stuttered, tried to apologize, and fell miserably silent.

Andrews' face hardened. "Glad you both had a good time," he said shortly. "All right. Report to the gun park. Drill in ten minutes."

Orders to move his platoon to Long Island with other units of Massachusetts field artillery lifted Andrews out of his gloomy abstraction. Cannoneers, guns, and teams, ferried across the East River, passed Brooklyn Heights, fortified by Washington's order since that high ground commanded New York as Dorchester did Boston. They joined troops on Long Island under Putnam, Sullivan, and Lord Stirling, the New Jerseyman who claimed a Scottish earldom. Mingling with regiments from other States, Andrews once more felt that sense of comradeship, of a common cause, that had come to him when New Yorkers helped bring the guns from Fort Ti. He admired particularly the soldierly bearing of the First Maryland in their fringed hunting shirts dyed purple, and the Delaware Blues whose smart uniforms resembled the artillery's. With the Delawares were two mascots, belligerent little gamecocks called the Blue Hen's Chickens, which beat all challengers matched against them by other outfits. The Blues, Andrews thought, would fight as gallantly as their roosters.

Battle lines drawn, an American force of 8,000 men confidently awaited the underrated foe. Men spoke proudly of Lexington and Concord, of Bunker Hill. If the Britishers were willing to pay a like price for Long Island trenches, let them have them. There would not be enough of them left to storm Brooklyn Heights and push on to take New

York. Around the campfires Andrews heard *Chester* sung again.

> When God inspired us for the fight,
>   Their ranks were broke, their lines were forced.
> Their ships were shelter'd in our sight,
>   Or swiftly driven from our coast.

But the British fleet, far from quitting the coast, sailed in closer to menace New York, and when General Howe's army made a surprise attack on the night of August 26th, it was the American ranks that were broken, American lines that were forced.

General Washington's army fell back into its main defenses. Tired fighting men shook their heads gloomily, then began to reassure themselves. You couldn't win every battle. These were formidable foes they were facing. That fact had been too easy to forget after chasing them out of Boston. British Regulars had to be admired as the real soldiers they were. And those German fellows—Hessians or Dutchmen or whatever they were—hired or not, they stood up to a scrap as if they had picked it themselves.

But they weren't fighting for their own country, and neither were the Redcoats, for it wasn't their country any more. This was the United States of America, free and independent as the great Declaration said, and it must be kept so. Tomorrow's battle must tell a different story.

In the lines the men of Andrews' battery were at last dismissed and ordered to sleep in their gun emplacements, ready for instant action. Every item of armament and equipment had been checked and rechecked. Private Connors growled wearily to Brooks:

"Sure and I've counted ivery linchpin and powder grain we've got. It's meself I've counted ten times, answering roll call. 'Tis a good thing the inimy doesn't know their up against ten Connors, or—"

"—they'd give up without a fight," Brooks added drily.

"It's right you are, Corp. Now by way of finishing up before we turn in I'd best call the roll of the guns, too. 'Mistress Lucy,' the Irishman snapped out and answered in a high falsetto, "Here, sor."

"Mind your tongue, Connors," Brooks warned him. "That gun's named for the Colonel's lady. And you'll show respect as well to 'Hancock' and 'Adams,' signers of the Declaration."

"Masters Hancock and Adams," Connors called out grinning. "You needn't be answering. I can see your worships are present." Then he went on in a subdued voice, " 'Saint Paul' is with us—and tomorrow may the saints preserve us!"

"And may we preserve the 'Saint,' " said Brooks.

CHAPTER IX

Stricken Field

HE four guns, flanked by Massachusetts infantry, covered a field over which part of the enemy attack must come this morning to follow up yesterday's success. As usual their bronze barrels shone, and lead-gray carriages had been washed clean. Elevating screws were oiled and axles well greased. Filled powder and water-buckets stood ready to hand. Besides the emergency ammunition in the side-boxes, rounds for immediate use were stacked in small caves hollowed out at the base of the parapet as protection from enemy shells dropped into the trench.

Kent Andrews scanned the intrenchments. At any rate they were stronger than the straw-bolstered rail fence on Breed's Hill, and the troops holding them were far better trained and armed. But there was no discounting British Regulars—not after the fight yesterday.

Andrews thought: If they break through here and drive us, we can fall back on the strong forts General Washington has had built at the foot of Long Island, where the East River cuts it off from Manhattan, and beat them back there.

Quickly he put the thought out of his mind. The idea of retreat sapped resolution. A soldier's duty was to stand and fight.

Yonder in the distance enemy ranks were forming, their uniforms not scarlet but blue. Andrews saw it was the Hessians who would strike the Massachusetts front. A major near him burst out angrily:

"Aye, Hessians," he confirmed. "Hirelings and slaves! Brought over by the British to take away our liberty—liberty they've never known themselves. King George pays seven pounds in blood money to their rulers for each one we kill and three pounds for the wounded. See to it today that it costs His Britannic Majesty plenty, Andrews. Sheep for the slaughter!"

But the Hessians advanced like soldiers, colors flying and drums beating a bass burden to the weird high notes of their hautboys or oboes. Now they were coming within artillery range.

Though twelve- as well as six-pounders had opened fire, the range was still too long for threes. Andrews, measuring with his eyes, sensed the eagerness of the gun crews awaiting his word. The Hessians came on, closing gaps in the ranks made by the shells of the heavier calibres. About 800 yards now; still too far, but worth a ranging shot. Andrews turned to Brooks on Number Four.

"Try one round, Corporal," he ordered. "Our first message to the Hessians."

Brooks, sighting along the barrel and giving a turn to the elevating screw, replied: "This being 'Saint Paul,' sir, I'll call that message an epistle to the Romans. Number Four, fire!"

The bombardier's match swept down to ignite the powder train to the vent. "Saint Paul" spoke.

"Short fifty yards," the battery commander estimated. He waited, letting the enemy approach to 600 yards. British artillery was booming now, firing over the heads of the assault troops. But they were overshooting the American trenches, and Andrews' men in their zeal to open up with their own guns paid no heed. At last he let them loose with a shout: "Two rounds. Fire!"

"First and Second Corinthians," Brooks yelled, as "Saint Paul" boomed twice, the other three guns chiming in with a roar.

Matrosses rolled them back into battery from the recoil. "Tend vent—Sponge pieces." Sergeants barked the familiar orders. Crews obeyed like clockwork. Months of gun drill were paying off. "Handle cartridge." Ammunition passers snatched up flannel bags of powder and rounds of shot and ran to the gaping muzzles. "Charge piece—Ram down cartridge." Loads were shoved in, driven home to the breech. "Prime." Gunners thrust tubes through vents into the cartridge and spilled a small gray-black train from powder horns. "Take aim," and corporals sighted anew and jumped clear, as bombardiers blew the slow matches on their linstocks into a red glow and stepped forward. Again the order to fire. Matches to powder trains. The sharp slams of the three-pounders beat against eardrums. Thick, choking smoke hid the field, but even deafened ears could hear screams and cries from the oncoming Hessians ranks, reeling under the deadly battering.

Now shells from enemy artillery began to burst around the battery. Not one of the American gun squads faltered. Load, aim, and fire—the steady, machine-like evolutions clicked on. Connors, plying his rammer-staff, grinned back over the muzzle at his lieutenant. All that drill Andrews had put them through made sense after all. If a man knew his duties, he did them, regardless. When you were being shot at, it helped to be serving a gun at top speed. You had no time to be scared.

More gaps had opened in the lines of the Hessians. They kept closing them up and marched steadily forward. Mercenaries, true enough, but warriors, brave men. Andrews could see them plainly now through the drifting smoke. Pipe-clayed crossbelts over blue coats, yellow waistcoats and breeches, black gaiters. Lofty, brass-mounted caps on hair tallowed and powdered with flour. Fierce, jutting, blackened mustachios giving an awesome, foreign look. American infantry poured volleys into them, but still they came on, hoarsely shouting their battle cry, *"Hoch! Hoch!"*

Andrews muttered, "We can stop them," and urged on his toiling gun crews. But the enemy counterbattery fire was growing heavier. Worse, it was crashing in from both flanks as well as from the front. Troops to their right and left must have given way. If the guns were to be saved, it was time to move them out. Andrews ordered dragropes fastened to haul the guns back to the teams and limbers, waiting in the shelter of a clump of trees.

Yankee infantry along the line still held despite the crossfire of shells. They fired a ragged volley. Before they could reload, the Hessians were on them, giving no quarter, bayoneting all who tried to surrender, and even the wounded. Andrews burned with sudden, wild hatred at the sight of such barbarity.

The four guns boomed on. Andrews heard Brooks wildly shouting something about epistles to the Galatians, Ephesians, and Philippians with every round of grape "Saint Paul" blasted out.

But they had stood their ground a little too long. Though three of the guns were clear and being dragged rapidly to the rear, an avalanche of Hessians descended on "Saint Paul." Most of its crew was down. Brooks lay slumped over the barrel.

A big Hessian leaped on the parapet. He swung his musket in an arc. His bayonet gleamed and darted downward to stab the stunned gunner. Andrews fired at him with his pistol and saw with anguish that he had missed. It was Sergeant Sampson who came to the rescue with a ferocious jab of a rammer-staff that caught the Hessian in the pit of the stomach. With a gasp he doubled up and collapsed. Sampson heaved the gunner over one shoulder and obeyed Andrews' shout to abandoned the gun and get out.

Back among the trees they limbered the three surviving guns and retreated at a trot, cannoneers following at a panting run. As they reached a rise of ground, they unlimbered and went into action again. Wreathed in battle smoke, they lost track of time and lived only for the moment. Stand and fight again. Blaze away in desperate rearguard action. Limber, pull out, then open up again on an enemy that never ceased harrying them, giving no respite. Fire till ammunition chests were empty. Guns impotent, cannoneers staggering with exhaustion, the artillery streamed back in the retreat of a shattered army, outgeneraled, outflanked, outfought. Valiant Marylanders and Delaware men took heavy losses, covering the rout. On the fields of Long Island lay the toll of defeat: hundreds of dead and wounded, with Generals Sullivan and Stirling and a thousand other prisoners in British hands.

Brooklyn Heights and their forts were a barrier, a refuge. Howe halted pursuit and mustered his victorious regiments to storm the works and gobble up the cornered Rebels. Tomorrow would be soon enough to deliver the assault.

But tomorrow would be too late. During the night, a night whose blackness and fogginess were providential, Washington withdrew his weary, beaten troops and sent them marching down to the East River.

Andrews swung his three guns into a long, dim column. From the rumbling of many other wheels and clop of hoofs he guessed that most of the rest of the field artillery had survived the battle. As far as he could make out, there were no heavy sling wagons or stone sledges. That meant that the siege cannon in the forts on the Heights were being abandoned. Well, it would be pure luck if all the infantry and field guns could cross over to New York before dawn.

Low-voiced orders were passed along the column. "Silence in the ranks. No talking. Muffle those trace chains." No warning must reach the British that Washington's army was slipping out of their grasp. The column halted, jammed up, then groped forward again. From up ahead came the sound of waves splashing against piles and the damp smell of the river. A staff officer rode up to the battery. "All right, you gunner officer. Your turn. Get your outfit aboard those boats and make it quick. There's three regiments in the fort still to cross."

It was a touchy business in the darkness—rolling guns

and ammunition carts across planks onto flat-bottomed scows, then leading nervous horses aboard. The poor beasts snorted in fright at the unsteady footing; drivers and matrosses had all they could do to control them.

"Tie them to the limber wheels," Andrews ordered, "but use slipknots. Jerk 'em loose if we capsize." He could not bear to think of the horses being dragged down and drowned. Freed, they could swim and perhaps reach shore. Let them have the same chance as he and his men, though it would be a slim one if they overturned in that wide, black river.

Sergeant Sampson, cradling the now-conscious Brooks in his arms, spoke softly from the second scow: "Lieutenant, it's Colonel Glover's men taking us across. We're in good hands."

Andrews knew the reputation of those Marblehead fishermen—first-rate boatmen and fighting men, too. But even in stormy seas they had not faced such a task as handling these awkward, heavy-laden craft. The scows swung into the current, tossing on the choppy water. The horses, sensing the peril, whinnied and stamped despite efforts of drivers at their heads to quiet them. Artillerymen crouched close to the thwarts, ready to swim for it if they capsized. To drown after surviving a hard-fought battle and lose the guns they had saved would be a doubly miserable fate.

Calmly and steadily the Marbleheaders plied their sweeps. They seemed to be able to see in the darkness, and strong strokes drove the scows forward unerringly. At last bows grated on the New York shore. A sergeant of Glover's called over:

"All ashore, Lieutenant. Got more ferrying to do tonight."

Andrews answered gratefully. "Sergeant," he said, "if I

ever have to get my guns over another river, I'd like to cross with you men."

"Count on us, sir. We'll be handy."

Before many months the artilleryman would welcome that offer at a vastly more difficult and dangerous crossing.

A surgeon had treated Gunner Brooks, in a house in New York. "This lad will be all right in no time. Took a glancing blow on his head, but it doesn't seem to have cracked his tough skull," the doctor told Andrews as he left.

Brooks looked up from his cot, and there were tears in the corners of his eyes. "I lost my gun, sir," he said quietly.

Andrews answered gently: "Through no fault of yours, Eph. I should have pulled out sooner. And thanks to Sampson, my best gunner was saved. I'll need you on one of the other guns. Cheer up now."

Brooks managed a weak grin. "Poor 'Saint Paul,'" he sighed. "He never had a chance to deliver the first and second epistles to the Thessalonians."

CHAPTER X

The Spy

THE American army had escaped from Long Island, but it could not hold New York town. It fell back fighting northward along Manhattan Island. Time and again it was almost cut off and crushed, slipping away only because the British pursuit was slow. Colonel Knox himself was almost trapped in a redoubt; at the last moment he got away by the one road still open. The Redcoats won the Battles of Harlem Heights and White Plains.

Fort Washington fell after a gallant defense, its garrison of 3,000 picked troops made prisoner and 114 pieces of artillery taken. When Cornwallis captured Fort Lee across the Hudson, thirty-two more precious cannon went the way of the others, along with sorely needed supplies.

90

In the bleak days of early December, 1776, a year which had begun so gloriously with the taking of Boston and was ending in such disaster, Washington again retreated with his beaten army through New Jersey and across the Delaware River to Pennsylvania.

To Lieutenant Andrews, obeying orders to report to the Chief of Artillery, that title seemed almost empty now, with all the American heavy ordnance and not a few of the field guns lost. But Knox greeted him with the same spirit he had always shown, and on a table lay the epaulettes of a brigadier general, proof that he had lost none of Washington's confidence. He waved aside Andrews congratulations.

"That commission has still to be confirmed by Congress, Kent. I haven't yet the right to wear those epaulettes."

"You will have, sir. You fully deserve them."

"After our defeats, all our losses?" Knox looked doubtful. "But my possible promotion wasn't why I sent for you. I have wonderful news for you. We've just heard that your Constancy is back in Boston again, safe and unharmed. One of our privateers caught that looter's brigantine before it could reach Halifax."

Andrews' joy and relief slowly gave way to the old ugly doubt. Was Constancy glad or sorry to come home? He would not learn until she wrote him—or be sure even then. A girl who might have planned an elopement with a British officer would not be likely to admit it when it failed to come off. Only a face-to-face meeting with Constancy could bring out the truth, Andrews thought, and leave from the army now was an impossibility. In these desperate days, with the ranks thinned by casualties, prisoners, expired enlistments, and desertions, a man who believed in the cause he was fighting for must stick to his guns.

"Your guns?" Knox asked, as if he had read his lieutenant's mind. "Are they in good condition?"

"Yes, sir. The three I have left are ready for action and ready to roll, if we have to retreat again."

"We're through retreating." Knox's voice was determined. "The Delaware River's between us and the enemy. General Washington took possession of all the boats along shore for many miles. Even if the British could build any, our Pennsylvania river navy would sink them as soon as they were launched."

"But when the river freezes and the ice is strong enough for Howe to cross?"

Knox, ignoring the question, went to the window and stared across the Delaware at the winter-bare New Jersey fields stretching away toward Trenton. "How did your guns and teams manage that night crossing of East River after Long Island?" he asked abruptly.

"Very handily, sir. No trouble."

"Good. That experience might be useful."

But experience would not be enough. They must know what lay ahead of them in the country held by the enemy beyond the Delaware River.

That was how Kent Andrews came to meet the spy.

John Honeyman, branded as a Tory traitor by his patriot neighbors, sat trussed by ropes to a chair in a house near Washington's headquarters. On guard over him, Lieutenant Kent Andrews faced the prisoner, a loaded pistol on the table before him. A sentry paced up and down in the hallway beyond the closed door.

With a dazed expression, Andrews stared at the man put in his charge by Washington's personal order. The General's amazing words still rang in his ears.

"Lieutenant, you are recommended to me by Colonel

Knox as a trustworthy and discreet officer who will obey orders without question. You will confine, and mount guard over, this prisoner, captured by one of our patrols across the river while he was gathering cattle to sell to the Hessians in Trenton. Tonight you will allow him to overpower you and make his escape. Tomorrow I shall publically reprimand you. You will accept it and say nothing of this to anyone at any time. I shall be grateful for your service. Take the prisoner away."

Evidently the General had extracted valuable information from the drover and was letting him go free as a reward, Tory though he was. But mightn't it have been wiser to hold him until the imminent move Knox had hinted at had been made?

By the light of a candle between them Andrews saw Honeyman regarding him with a grin. The fellow addressed him in a low voice.

"It'll be a while yet, Lieutenant, afore it's dark enough for you to let me fly the coop. A little gab might pass the time. Ever been to Trenton?"

"No."

"Pretty town. The Hessians holding it like it fine. Snug in winter quarters there, they are—a whole brigade of 'em, Colonel Rall commanding. He has his own grenadiers and the Knyphausen and Lossberg regiments, Jaegers and some British dragoons, too. They've got pickets out but don't bother much with patrols to the river."

Honeyman knew how to use his eyes, Andrews thought. No wonder General Washington had welcomed his news.

"Nope, too cold to patrol," Honeyman went on. " 'Sides, those Dutchmen don't think much of you Rebels. Ever heard what they say about you? Never mind. Guess it don't bear repeating."

"Go ahead. Let's have it."

"Well, they claim that all American officers were just tailors, barbers, laborers, or shopkeepers before they joined the army."

"Some truth in that. General Greene has skill as a blacksmith. Colonel Knox sold books. I was his assistant."

"They claim your regiments look like a crowd of beggars and scarecrows."

"True, and more's the pity. You've seen for yourself. We're ragged and hungry. Too many of our lads have worn-out shoes or only sacking wrapped around their feet."

"They say that most of you would surrender if you weren't scared of being hanged for treason."

"Why, those low-down—"

Honeyman interrupted, hiding a grin: "They say that your artillery is wretched stuff—that it's mostly scrap-iron barrels mounted on ship-gun carriages."

"Blast their eyes! I've been living for the day our guns can open on those devils again and blow them off the face of the earth! I saw Hessians bayonet our wounded and prisoners on Long Island."

The other turned grave. "I heard about that. I'm making no excuses for them, Lieutenant, but they'd been told by the British that you people, like the Injuns, scalped and ate your enemies. Simpletons of their rank and file believe it."

"You've been dealing with them—selling them beef."

"A man has to make a living," Honeyman answered with a shrug. "I sell 'em cattle. Others sell 'em rum. Never saw so many barrels of it as they've got rounded up in Trenton. Christmas is coming, and the Hessians make a revel of it. They'll start guzzling it Christmas Eve and be at it all Christmas day and night. Old Rall can drink the best of 'em under the table. Late mornings he sobers up enough to inspect guard mount and listen to his band serenade him. Never heard finer music myself. Trumpets, clarinets, and hautboys. Trenton youngsters love it."

"I heard Colonel Rall fought well when they took Fort Washington from us."

"Might have. Now he's taking his liquor and his ease, playing checkers and cards. I see by your uniform that you're an artilleryman, Lieutenant. Ought to have taken note of that 'fore I passed on that dig of the Hessians about your guns."

"Yes, I'm an artilleryman."

"Hessians have some right smart-looking cannon. Six brass three-pounders. Got 'em lined up single file, one behind t'other, in King Street which is kind of narrow."

"But that's tarnal foolishness. That way they'd have a hard time bringing them into action."

"I wouldn't know, Lieutenant. I'm no soldier. But it seemed sort of queer to me that they've built no redoubt at the crossroads above King and Queen Streets. A man could stand there and roll balls down those two streets like they were bowling greens. If the balls were cannon balls . . ."

Andrews' stared harder. "Look here, Honeyman. You know plenty. Of course you told all this to General Washington."

"Well, I did make mention of it."

Andrews' growing suspicion crystalized. Undoubtedly Honeyman was an American spy and a corking good one. Undetected, he would be useful to Washington again.

"If you weren't tied up, I'd shake your hand, Honeyman," he said warmly. "You're doing first-rate work, dangerous work."

Honeyman bowed his head gravely. "Thanks. It's all right for me but a bit hard on my family, having folks call me a Tory and a traitor.

"Well, Lieutenant, time I'm off. With your unofficial help, I'll untie myself. . . . There, that's good. Ropes cramp the limbs. Afore I leave by that window I'd best overpower you like the General said. Ought to be convincing-like. For both our sakes this business mustn't look strange. Can't have a struggle, can we? Sentry would hear."

Andrews stood up and handed over his pistol. "I'll go out and speak to the sentry," he said. "When I come back and close the door, tap me on the head with the butt of this."

"Sorry, guess I'll have to." Honeyman smiled ruefully. "Good thing I'm a butcher. I know just how hard to hit a critter and only stun without breaking a skull. Luck to you, sir."

"And to you." Andrews went out, returned, and shut the door carefully behind him. A muffled blow crashed against his forehead, and he fell unconscious.

General Washington's stern reproof, anticipated though it was, was not easy to bear, nor was the contempt in the eyes of his listening staff. Andrews, standing at attention, with a bloody bandage around his head, heard the General finish, "For neglect of duty you are relieved of your command."

Andrews swayed on his feet and turned paler. Not to serve with his guns in the battle ahead! That was far worse punishment then he had expected. But he bit his lip and said nothing.

Henry Knox stepped forward. "General," he pleaded, "this young officer has never before failed me. I beg your

Excellency to give him an opportunity to redeem himself in action. If not with his guns, by serving on my staff."

Washington gave him a curt nod. "Very well, Colonel Knox, since you request it."

"Follow me, Andrews," Knox ordered and strode away. At some distance from the group he turned. One of his small gray eyes winked. So he knew! Andrews sighed with relief.

Knox said softly, "Bravely endured, Kent. You'll act as my aide when we cross the Delaware tonight."

Chapter XI

Dry Powder

$\mathbb{S}$NOW, sleet, hail, and bitter cold. The river crossing this Christmas night was infinitely more difficult than the escape from Long Island to Manhattan, and the need for haste was as great now as then. Twenty-four hundred men and eighteen cannon must be ferried over and march nine miles to Trenton before dawn, if the Hessian garrison was to be surprised. To fail could mean disaster. Washington's password was well chosen—"Victory or death."

Glover's Marblehead regiment manned the oars again. Without those fishermen-soldiers the passage could never be managed, thought Andrews, watching the infantry vanguard board boats shoved off into the dark river where jagged ice cakes swirled in the swift current. Beating his arms against his shivering body to warm it, he jumped at the sound of a mighty bellow.

"Forrest's guns next." That was Knox's great voice—none like it in the army. He stood at Washington's side, repeating his orders. Andrews ran to bring up the Pennsylvania battery. It was not hard to manhandle the cannon onto the long Durham boat, but the horses gave trouble. No one could blame the poor beasts for distrusting the unsteady footing on craft bobbing on the icy river. They balked and kicked. Men coaxed, then pulled and hauled, using whips when they had to, or shoving against haunches with boards. Above the storm, the thud of hoofs on planking, and the yelling of drivers, Knox's shout was heard urging them to hurry.

More infantry, more artillery—Alexander Hamilton's New York guns, Moulder's of Philadelphia, Neil's from New Jersey, a Massachusetts battery under Captain Winthrop Sargent. Washington had not been sparing of the cannon he would take into the battle ahead.

Now it was time for the General himself to embark. As he took his place, Knox followed and settled his bulk on a seat behind, his weight making the boat tip to the side. Before they shoved off, Andrews, from the shore, heard Washington crack one of his rare jokes: Knox, shift that fat bottom of yours and trim the ship."

Andrews, finding his horse, crossed with the Philadelphia Light Horse Troop. Short of the farther bank, their barge grounded on a shoal. Without hesitation the daring cavalrymen jumped their horses into the river and swam them ashore. But Andrews' mount refused, and he was forced to wait until the boat was freed and rowed on.

It was growing dangerously late, for the crossing had taken three hours. Andrews spurred after the army, its path marked by dark blotches on the snow: bloody footprints of poorly shod soldiers. He overtook a marching

column of sleet-soaked infantrymen. Ahead two guns
slithered behind weary teams, with gunners, who had
harnassed themselves into hauling straps called bricoles,
helping the horses. A familiar voice hailed him, Captain
Hamilton's. Like his men, the New Yorker was walking,
now and then patting the barrel of one of his cannon, as
was his habit. His own mount was hitched in with a straining tandem.

"That you, Andrews?" Hamilton called. "Colonel Knox
was asking for you. Get on as fast as you can."

Slogging infantry again, leading elements of this first of
the two columns pressing on to attack Trenton. There rode
Washington on a sorrel charger and Knox on a big bay.
Andrews, coming up, heard a captain report that his company's powder was wet and the tall Virginian's sharp reply,
"You've got bayonets, haven't you? Use them!" Knox called
to his aide, "Andrews, tell Forrest to put his guns in position at the crossroads as soon as the enemy pickets are
driven in. And warn him to keep his powder dry."

Wet weather was artillery weather. In such snow and
sleet as were falling tonight, infantrymen's efforts to protect the firing mechanism of their muskets by wrapped
rags availed little; before they could fire, powder in priming pans would be sodden and flints too damp to spark.
Gunners, with cartridges kept in covered side-boxes and
ammuntion chests, could load and shield powder trains to
primers until matches touched them off. This battle—its
outset at least—would be an affair of cannon and bayonets.

Suddenly the sky was gray, then light. Up ahead Andrews saw a Hessian officer saunter out of a farmhouse,
sight the American advance, and yell for his men. They
rushed forth, fired a few scattered shots, and fled back
toward Trenton before the threat of swooping bayonets.

Ragged infantry charged after them, and gun teams took up a trot.

Hoarse shouting rose in the town. *"Der Fiend! Heraus, heraus!"* "The enemy! Turn out!" Streets filled with the German mercenaries, dull with sleep and fuddled by rum, struggling into coats and equipment. Yelling officers shoved their men into ranks, trying to form line for volleys. The yellow metal fronts of grenadier caps reflected the early morning light, and uniforms splashed color against the snowy background—Rall's regiment and the Lossbergers both in the blue, the former with facings of poppy color, the latter's of orange. In marked contrast was the somber black worn by the Knyphausens. Here and there a flash of green with crimson trim identified the Jaegers, sons of German foresters and deadly shots with their short, heavy rifles.

Four of Forrest's guns came into action, raking crowded King Street. Now Hamilton's battery was up and ready to fire, Knox himself giving the range. Its shells caught the Lossbergers flooding into Queen Street and smashed them back. Cannon boomed also from the other side of town where the second American column had launched its assault.

Bursts of smoke and flame and sharp reports answered from the head of Queen Street. The Hessians at last had managed to bring two of their three-pounders to bear, but they were able to fire only eight rounds before a blast of counterbattery from the crossroads hit them. German artillerymen reeled back, dragging one gun with them. The other, half its crew and three horses killed, was abandoned.

American infantry, their way cleared by the gunners, charged down the slope into town, shouting a strange battle cry: "These are the times that try men's souls!" That was from Tom Paine's pamphlet, *Crisis*, which had been read to the troops a few days before and stirred them deeply. Andrews, riding after them while the guns limbered to follow, saw a captain, William Washington, shot through both hands but never faltering, lead his company in its rush. His lieutenant was struck in the left shoulder by a bullet that severed an artery. Clamping the wound with a strong grip of his right hand that stopped the spurting blood, he, too, kept dashing on in the charge that captured two Hessian guns. Andrews, recognizing the wounded lieutenant, would recall this moment years later when the brave officer, James Monroe, became President of the United States.

Musketeers and riflemen forced their way into houses. Soon lead spat from windows, mowing down the rallying Hessians. The Americans, under cover from the wet, had loaded and primed with dry powder from their horns and chipped damp flakes from their flints. Their sniping fire was deadly.

Colonel Rall, roused from his bed when the attack he had contemptuously discounted was already breaking his fine brigade, rode furiously through the disordered mass of fugitives, striving to stem the retreat. He had succeeded in making a stand, and his grenadiers were advancing with band playing and colors flying, when a fusilade drove them staggering back. Rall fell from his horse, mortally wounded. Unread in his pocket was a note, sent Christmas night by a Tory, to warn him that the Americans were crossing the Delaware to storm Trenton.

Lashed by rifle and artillery fire, dismayed by the loss of their commander, the Hessians fell back. Some escaped to Bordentown, but most were cut off by the two columns converging on them. Yet they were still formidable and,

fighting hard to hold pursuers in check, companies retreated to fields and orchards around the town. Ranks
formed and stiffened under long-familiar discipline.
Though pouring rain drenched powder-pans, the Hessian
infantry stood at bay with bristling bayonets. Lossberg
artillerymen struggled to extricate their two cannon,
bogged down in a swamp, and reply to the Massachusetts
battery, firing on them from high ground to the south.

Knox's deep bass summoned Andrews, and boomed an
order for Sargent's, Neil's, and Moulder's guns to limber
up and close in. Saluting, the aide pushed his weary mount
as fast as he could through the snow and mud. As he
rounded the corner of a farmhouse, a tall Hessian grenadier stepped out, leveled his musket, and pulled the trigger. The hammer clicked harmlessly—wet powder—but the
American's horse, swerving in fright, slipped and went
down. Andrews, supine, looked up at fierce blue eyes and
a flashing bayonet thrusting down at his chest. Frantically
he rolled to one side, not quite quickly enough. The bayonet, gashing his shoulder, plunged into the ground. Before
the Hessian could wrench it out, Andrews was on his feet,
the sword he had never used in his hand. He parried the
now withdrawn bayonet, lunged, and heard a groan as
his blade drove home. Faint and sick, he staggered toward
his horse which had regained its feet but had not run
away. He dragged himself up into the saddle and rode on.

Later he found himself standing, half-dazed by fatigue
and loss of blood, behind the cannon he had brought.
Loaded with grape, gunners ready with their slow matches,
the guns ringed the Hessians in orchard and swamp with
a deadly semicircle. Infantry, poised to charge, thronged
around them. General St. Clair shouted, "Surrender or
we'll blow you to pieces!"

The trapped enemy stared up at those menacing black muzzles. Surrender or annihilation—they had no other choice. Andrews saw proud silken standards of the German States lowered to droop in the muddy snow. Arms thudded to the ground, and officers, as a sign of submission, held up their hats on the points of their swords.

Almost a thousand prisoners, more than a hundred enemy casualties, six cannon and many other munitions and supplies captured—and all at the cost of four Americans wounded. It was a great victory and would have been greater still if other troops Washington had ordered to cross the river farther along had not failed to do so. Yet this day had restored hope to the American cause, a cause so nearly lost.

Andrews remembered little of the army's return to Pennsylvania. He recalled only that a surgeon had dressed his wound and he had been put to bed in Knox's quarters. When he woke after a long sleep, he saw his chief writing at a table near the window. The big man, noticing he was awake, came over and took his hand in an affectionate grasp.

"My pride in you is great, Kent," he said. "Your gallantry is being mentioned in orders. They will redeem you in the eyes of others for permitting the escape of the 'Tory'." He called to an orderly in the kitchen that the Lieutenant was ready for breakfast.

"I've been studying what reward to give you, Kent," Knox went on. "You amply deserve one. But I can't promote you. There's no vacancy at present. And I take that hard since my own promotion has now come through. Congress has confirmed me as a brigadier general with the entire command of the artillery."

"Heartiest congratulations, sir! That delights me more than any greater rank for myself possibly could."

"You were ever loyal and generous, Kent. Yet I'm still at a loss on what I can do in your behalf."

"I've a request, sir."

"Name it. I'll grant it if I can, as you well know."

"Then, sir, give me one of the Hessian three-pounders we took at Trenton for my battery. They're first-rate guns. It would replace the one I lost on Long Island."

Knox beamed. "Kent, it's yours," he said. "I'll issue the order."

"All my thanks, Colonel— I mean General. Sorry, sir."

"I'm not used to my new rank, either," Knox answered, grinning. "Well, that's settled—all except christening the gun. I've no doubt you plan that."

"Already had a name in mind, in case I got the gun," Andrews confessed. "Of course, it's German. And you'll remember those books you had in the shop—books you recommended I read—about a German king and fine general who was a master at handling artillery."

"Frederick the Great, no less!" Knox exclaimed. "So that's the name you've chosen?"

"Yes, sir, if that's all right."

"Eminently all right. A splendid artilleryman, of whatever nation, is worthy of honor. So you'll have your 'Frederick the Great' speaking to the Hessian hirelings from the realm he once ruled. And to the Redcoats, too."

"In strong language, sir."

So a new piece joined Andrews' battery. The guns were four again.

Chapter XII

The Guns Go to College

KNOX had forty cannon under his command now. For the first time since he had brought the guns from Fort Ti he outmatched the Royal Artillery. The big General was especially eager to face his proud opponents whose motto was *Ubique*—Everywhere— since they had served in many parts of the world.

Telling his gunner officers about the motto, Knox said: "Very well, let them make their boast that they've fought everywhere. We'll meet them anywhere."

They met again at Trenton. General Cornwallis marched against Washington, vowing "to bag the fox" that had taken the town from his Hessians in the first American victory since Boston. British dragoons tauntingly sounded the old fox-hunting call, "View Halloo" on their trumpets as they rode into battle.

Guns blazed across the Jersey fields. Kent Andrews, still weak from his wound, commanded his battery on horseback. He knew that if his mount were hit, he could not walk far, yet he had no fear of being left to be captured. Sergeant Sampson's eyes were on him when enemy shells burst near the battery. Andrews was certain that if he or his horse were hit, he would be carried clear by the strong non-com, as Brooks had been on Long Island.

All day they fought the Redcoats to a standstill. That night General Washington ordered campfires left burning while his army slipped away. Artillerymen muffled the wheels of their gun carriages in rags so that they rolled away without any telltale rumbling. Even the drivers, usually a noisy lot with their teams, kept silence. When the British awoke next morning, they gaped at an empty American camp. Washington had led his army around their left flank and was marching hard to strike their rear guard at Princeton and their supply base at New Brunswick.

Conflict raged south of the town. Cheering Americans drove back the enemy pickets and struck the main line hard. It wavered and almost broke. Then Andrews saw a British colonel ride forward with two little spaniels frisking at his horse's heels. Gallantly he rallied his men. They swept forward in a charge. At the side of Neil's New Jersey guns, Andrews' battery sprayed the enemy with canister. Red ranks wilted but re-formed and came on. A few minutes more and they would engulf the American cannon. Andrews realized that he must act fast or he would lose not only one gun, as on Long Island, but all four.

"Limber to the rear. Pull out!" he shouted.

Teams trotted up through the white clouds of battle smoke. Crews hooked on the pieces. In a trice they were

clear and dashing out at a gallop. But Neil and his cannoneers had stayed too long. Overrun, they flailed away at
the foe with rammer staffs and handspikes until they died
around their guns under musket shots and bayonet thrusts.

Now Andrews and his men put the four guns into action
again, taking position to the right of Moulder's Pennsylvania battery. Once more it was touch and go, with British
infantry and cavalry pressing them hard and working
around the flanks. Slowly the guns gave ground, hauled
back by dragropes—then halted to blast the foe with grape
and canister. Only the valiant little troop of Philadelphia
Light Horse saved them, blocking the enemy pursuit to
give the artillery a respite.

It was when Andrews realized in despair that they could
not stand and fight much longer that he looked over his
shoulder. He would never forget the splendid sight he
saw. General Washington burst through the smoke on a
chestnut charger at full gallop. He rode to within forty
paces of the enemy. A point-blank volley flamed at him,
but the tall figure was unhit. Washington waved on the
infantry regiments rushing onto the field after him. Nothing could stop their furious assault. Supported by the fire
of the cannon, they shattered the British ranks and hurled
them back in headlong retreat. As they ran, Andrews heard
General Washington's exultant shout:

"It's a fine fox chase, boys!"

The Battle of Princeton was won, but the enemy must
be allowed no rest.

A battery of the New York artillery whirled onto the
road leading to the town. Andrews, hailed by its short,
handsome captain, recognized Alexander Hamilton.

"Kent," Hamilton called over, "can you follow me with

your battery? We're going to chase the Lobster-backs out of Princeton town."

"Be right behind you, sir," Andrews replied.

The two batteries swung around a handsome brick building in Princeton, unlimbered, and placed their guns so that their fire could cover it from every angle. Musket barrels poked from all its windows, and the doors appeared to be barred and barricaded. Here was a stronghold in which part of the British rearguard was prepared to make a stand and hold up pursuit while the remnants of the main body made good their escape.

Hamilton waved a hand toward the building. "That," he said, "is Nassau Hall of the College of New Jersey."

"You've been here before?" Andrews asked.

"Yes. I planned to enter as a student, but they refused me. I went instead to King's College in New York, nor have I ever regretted it."

Andrews shook his head over an institution's declining such a brilliant young man as Alexander Hamilton.

Hamilton, smiling, added: "I might make a delayed entrance now, with the help of some cannon balls, but I'm afraid that would show unbecoming resentment. Besides we can't batter down those stout walls with just my four— and six-pounders and your threes. Are you prepared for action, Kent?"

"Yes, sir. Ready to fire."

"Two of my guns bear on the main door. I think we can batter it in. You have the rear door covered in case the Lobster-backs try to break out there?"

"I have, sir. Two guns. One loaded with round shot, one with canister. And my two other guns cover the windows on this side."

"Be ready to fire at my word."

"Very good, sir."

Gunner Brooks, with "Frederick the Great" trained on one of the windows, called to his lieutenant.

"The Captain say this was a college, sir?"

"That's right."

Brooks grinned. "Couldn't be more fitting," he said. "Three of our guns have already been to school in Boston under Master Holbrook. Now they're going to college."

Hamilton had walked over to them. "I'd like to try one round from this piece first," he decided. "Right through that window. By your leave, Gunner." He bent over and checked the laying. "Good. Bombardier, fire!"

"Frederick" crashed. The round shot plunged through the window. An instant later a shot from one of Hamilton's guns thudded into the brick façade of Nassau Hall between the second and third stories, leaving a dent that has been preserved to this day through all reconstructions of the building.

It was too much for the British defenders who expected to have the walls tumble down upon them. Waving a white rag, two hundred of them came pouring out the doors to surrender.

The minute after Nassau Hall had been vacated by the enemy, Brooks rushed in to see the result of the shot through the window. Back he raced to report his news with great glee.

"Got a direct hit on a big painting of a king!" he shouted. "Right through the royal noggin. 'Off with his head!' says Captain Hamilton, and we obliged. Can't say I recognized who it was after that, but a sign under the picture said George the Second."

Andrews identified the portrait. "Grandfather of the present King of Great Britain."

"Aha!" Brooks crowed. "I'm moved to a speech. Somebody's else's speech but a good one." He struck an attitude and grandly declaimed. "'And George the Third may profit by his example!'"

"That was Patrick Henry's speech," Andrews said.

"Thank you, sir. So it was. And what else was it he said? Oh, yes." The gunner turned toward the group of sullen British prisoners with a defiant, "'If that be treason, make the most of it!'"

Sergeant Sampson snorted. "Dry up, Brooks. They're not fixed to make the most of anything right now."

There was no stopping the enthusiastic gunner. "Fi, Sergeant," he chided. "You have no imagination. Lieutenant Andrews, didn't you say this was a college? Well, it occurs to me that our four guns have just graduated. And with high honors. The Latin phrase for it escapes me."

Sampson said wryly, "I'll tell you what else escapes you, Brooks. A lot of long-winded babbling."

"The Latin you want is *magna cum laude*," Andrews supplied.

"That's it, sir. I'd ask Sergeant Sampson to present the diplomas, but he doesn't seem to rise to the spirit of the occasion. We'll have to make do with a graduation ode. Give me a moment. Ah, I have it. Lend me your ears."

Surrounded by grinning artillerymen, Brooks recited:

> Our cannon ball, its aim well reckoned,
> Cut off the head of George the Second.
> When of our guns abroad they've heard,
> We'll win the war from George the Third.

CHAPTER XIII

Spirit of Artillerymen

WASHINGTON'S troops made a winter encampment in Morristown, New Jersey. From that strong position they watched the British, pent up in New Brunswick, Perth Amboy, and New York after the glorious American victories at Trenton and Princeton.

Now Continental artillery regiments were formed, three of them for combat and one of artificers to keep the guns in repair. More cannon were being cast at the arsenal Knox was establishing at Springfield, Massachusetts, and at other foundries. Horses were drawn from stock confiscated from Tories, who would otherwise have sold them to the enemy. That had happened on Long Island where farmers took British gold to fill out the teams of the Royal Artillery.

Sticks rattled on drumheads all day as drill signals for

cannoneers and infantrymen, while trumpets blew for the
cavalry. Andrews, along with Sergeant Sampson, Corporal
Brooks, and Connors, kept recruits busy in the snow-cov-
ered artillery park. They were intelligent and eager, these
young fellows. All of them had hunted with rifles or fowling pieces but none had seen a cannon before with the
exception of one youth, still in his early teens. He had
made a cruise with a privateer as a powder boy. The most
reluctant of all the recruits, he was obviously unhappy at
being ashore and serving in the artillery.

Sergeant Sampson came down on him hard.

"You there, sprout!" he barked. "Hop to it! Think you're
still a sailor? Well, you ain't."

"That's just the trouble," the lad muttered sullenly.

Sampson growled at him, like a big dog at an impudent
puppy. "Oho! I figured that was it. You want to be back
taking your ease on a nice, comfortable ship. Don't care
for marching, do you? Don't like sleeping in a cold tent
or in the open under a gun carriage. Want to be back in a
warm bunk below decks, huh?"

The boy answered him stoutly. " 'T ain't that, Sergeant,"
he said, "nor yet the scant vittles. It's the pay. I haven't
seen a shilling yet. And I hear tell that if we do get paid,
't ain't much."

Sampson was silenced for a moment. It was true that
despite General Washington's pleas to Congress, pay for
the army was months in arrears. But the sergeant was
quick to speak again.

"So it's money you're fighting for. Not for your country.
Not for liberty."

"No!" The recruit looked the big non-com straight in the
eyes. "We got paid on the privateer, certain—well paid.
Even a powder monkey like me got his rightful share of

the prize money on enemy ships we took. I sent mine home. My mother's alone on the farm and hard put to make ends meet. All I want is something to help her with."

Now Sampson had no words, and Brooks stepped in. "I guess there's more than one of us understands trouble like that. But cheer up. Lieutenant Andrews has it from Headquarters that pay's coming in soon. Meanwhile we need your ship's gun experience, matross. All right, you'll act as bombardier. What are your duties?"

"To tend the vent," the boy answered promptly. "To carry the tube box, powder horn, and linstock. I clear the vent with my priming wire and pierce the cartridge in the bore. I prime the vent with a tube or powder from this horn." He slapped the big artillery powder horn, about ten times the size of a rifleman's.

"First-rate!" Both Sampson and Brooks spoke their praise at once.

"After we've fired," the boy went on, "I stop the vent like this"—he pressed the palm of his left hand down on the opening—"while the piece is charged."

"Why?" Sampson prompted.

"Some powder grains from the old charge might still be burning in the bore. Air through the vent would make them flare up and set off the new charge while it was being rammed in."

"And then?"

"It'd blow off the arms of the rammer-staff man."

"Good thing for you, you rammers, he knows that," Sampson put in.

A recruit asked, "Why's he wearing that leather pad? His hands soft?"

The former powder-monkey looked at him pityingly. "You try stopping the vent of a red-hot gun without this pad. Get the skin of your palm scorched right off, you will!"

Sergeant Sampson beamed. "We've got a new bombardier," he said. "That's more pay for you, lad—when we get it."

Rapidly now the gun crews began to pick up their duties and perform them, first at the word of command, then by taps of the drum.

Brooks, slapping the breach of the three-pounder, told his pupils: "This is just a light piece. You lads are in luck. When I was a recruit, I had to wrestle with a swamping, big thirteen-inch mortar. All you have to do is manhandle this featherweight."

"What are our horses for?" a husky recruit demanded brashly.

"To give you a horse laugh when you're inside a bricole, which is man harness, and pulling the gun instead of them," Brooks retorted. "All right, get hitched now, you. The rest of you on the dragropes. Pieces advance, hup!"

They hauled the gun forward until they were ordered to halt and prepare for action. Connors—there was no sterner drillmaster than that coverted grumbler—took over.

"You're out there in front of the piece, swabbin' out the bore," he told a young matross. "Your back's turned to the inemy comin' at you with a bayonet charge. What are you after thinkin'? What a pincushion feels like? NO! You does your duty and takes your post. Your mate here, not thinkin' neither, rams down the charge and takes his post. Gunner fires. By then the two of you are facin' front with a fine view of what grape or canister does to infantry chargin' right up to the muzzle."

"What do we do then?" one of the new men asked.

"Be thankful you're in the artill'ry," Connors snapped.

Andrews, who had been silently watching the drill, grinned. That was the right idea. You had to make a soldier keen about his own arm of the service. Undoubtedly the infantry drillmasters in the next field were telling their recruits how lucky they were to be foot troops, with only a musket to carry and no heavy cannon to pull out of the mud, no horses to water and feed before you could cook and eat your own rations. They'd be boasting that artillery was only for support—that it took infantry to win and hold ground.

Well, that was true, Andrews admitted to himself, but he could make these men of his as proud to serve with the guns. He could inspire them with stories of artillery's gallant feats. Give them pride in their arm, *esprit de corps,* and they would always stand by their guns in battle.

So in the evenings, after mess, Andrews talked to groups around a campfire about the Swedish king, Gustavus Adolphus, who won great victories by the massed fire of his fast-moving batteries, and about Frederick the Great who pushed his fieldpieces forward to point-blank range to open the way for the infantry. One of their cannon, he reminded them, was named for that monarch. He spoke, too, of the formidable adversary that Americans must meet gun to gun, the Royal Artillery.

He told them about Seth Pomeroy, who had fought at the siege of Louisbourg in 1745, where American artillery saw its first major action. It was Pomeroy who had unspiked the guns in the Grand Battery, captured by the Colonials, and turned them against the French. Thirty years later the veteran had volunteered for the defense of Bunker Hill. As he trudged up to the battle line, General Putnam hailed him: "You here, Pomeroy! A cannon shot would waken you out of your grave!" Only a short time ago, Andrews added, brave old General Pomeroy, seventy-one but still marching to the sound of the guns, had died at Peekskill on his way to join the army here at Morristown.

Flames flickered lower in the fire. Drums soon would beat "Tattoo." Andrews finished by telling the recruits the story of Trenton and the semicircle of cannon that forced surrender of the Hessians in the orchard, and of the last stand of Moulder's battery at Princeton. At the end, the faces of the young cannoneers were shining, and Andrews was content. In these men of his was the stuff that made artillerymen.

CHAPTER XIV

Blood in Brandywine Creek

WINTER gave way to spring, and spring to summer, and the fighting flared up again, as Howe sent out raiding columns, and Washington countered, driving them back. There were short, sharp clashes, affairs of regiments or brigades, accompanied by a gun or two. Was Howe feinting toward the Rebel capital, Philadelphia? If so, his thrusts were parried so vigorously that he made no effort in force to batter his way down through New Jersey and Pennsylvania. For weeks no sign of a Redcoat was seen by watchful American pickets.

In the port of New York, Admiral Howe's transports were taking his brother's army aboard: splendid regiments of English Regulars, Highlanders, Hessians—engineer trains of pontoons and wagons—fieldpieces and horses of

118

the Royal Artillery, with 300 rounds per gun and a reserve of 6,000 shells.

American spies sent word that two hundred and eleven vessels had set sail—warships and troop-carriers. But not until that great armada was sighted moving up Chesapeake Bay could Washington be certain that the enemy's objective was Philadelphia. Hastily he mustered his divisions for the city's defense.

Howe's army landed in Maryland, took its good time to recuperate from the voyage and to forage, then marched north through Delaware on Philadelphia. At Chad's Ford on Brandywine Creek on September 11, 1777, Washington barred the path and gave battle.

Andrews, ordered to support one of Sullivan's brigades, put his guns in position. The afternoon sun glinted on "Frederick the Great's" barrel, embossed with the arms of Hesse. It must do good service today against its former owners or the British. Crews stood alert at their posts. Andrews glanced at the young matrosses. They were pale— so he must have looked, he remembered, before his first action at Bunker Hill—but their eyes were bright and eager. They would not fail him. All was well in the woods to the rear where drivers and teams waited with the limbers and ammunition carts. One of the horses had cast a shoe that morning, but Andrews had managed to have it reshod at a handy traveling forge of Proctor's Artillery.

Yonder the enemy was deploying for the attack, long ranks of scarlet uniforms and green—guards on the right, grenadiers in the center, light infantry and Jaegers, Hessian sharpshooters, on the left. A band struck up to play them into action. Andrews recognized the martial strains of *The Grenadiers' March*. Words he knew pounded through his head.

Some talk of Alexander, and some of Hercules,
Of Hector and Lysander, and such great names as these;
But of all the world's great heroes, there's none that can
 compare
With a tow row row row row row, to the British Gren-
 adier.

Vaunting words, boastful words, but those tall men in
scarlet, taller still in their high bearskin caps, lived up to
them. They charged with the bayonet, never firing a shot.
Andrews' three-pounders slammed, their sharp reports
punctuating the musketry volleys rippling along the American line. Gaps opened in the scarlet ranks. They closed up,
came on. Off to their flanks the Royal Artillery thundered,
and twelve-pounder shells crashed down on the defense.

Two of Sullivan's brigades broke before the oncoming
charge. Lord Stirling's division, both flanks thus exposed,
streamed back in retreat. Officers strove vainly to stage a
rally. Foremost among them was the young Marquis de
Lafayette, recently come from France to help the American cause. The tall redhead, in spite of a bullet hole
through one leg, had dismounted from his horse and was
limping about, waving his sword toward the enemy. But
men whose cartridges were almost gone would not listen.
They fled before the gleaming British bayonets and the
plunging shells.

As the line melted away, Andrews yelled an order. He
must limber up and pull out to save his guns. Up whirled
the gun teams, but while one piece was being limbered,
the driver was hit by a shell fragment and slumped to the
ground. His terrified team would have bolted, if Brooks
had not instantly swung up into the empty saddle and
grasped the reins. Jouncing and rattling over the rough

ground, the gun carriage and ammunition chest raced away, the crew dashing after them.

General Greene was coming up to the rescue now, his leading brigade having covered four miles in forty minutes. They opened ranks, let the fugitives through, closed again—then stood fast and at fifty paces blasted back the onrushing grenadiers with deadly fire.

Breathless and leg-weary, Andrews and his men at last overtook their runaway guns. They brought them into action again beside others to the north of the ford where Anthony Wayne's brigade was fighting desperately to plug a gap in the line. Again the American cannon traded shells with enemy artillery whose smoke, thick and masking, drifted over the battleground. Fire. Load and fire again. Fire blindly. There was nothing else to do.

Water was low in the three-pounders' buckets, and there was no time to fill them at the creek. Not much longer could the swabbers cool steaming barrels, but they would keep firing until the guns burst. An overwhelming pride in his crews, in all his young matrosses, filled Andrews' heart.

Through the battle haze he thought he distinguished the scarlet uniforms with blue facings of the Royal Welch Fusiliers, advancing to attack. Was David Thorpe leading his platoon against him once more as at Bunker Hill?

Andrews never found out. Shrouded by smoke, his gun and the others in the line kept blazing away. Suddenly the infantry between them was gone, and the Redcoats were upon them, overrunning the position. Brooks brought up one team, but there was no chance to limber and escape now. Combat raged around the guns. Connors and a recruit beside him, jabbing to the last with rammer staffs, went down under a bristling hedge of British bayonets. Andrews, his sword arm numbed by the blow of a musket butt, found Sergeant Sampson clearing a space around him. The big man was wielding a trail handspike, laying about him with the fury of the Biblical Samson smiting the Philistines with the jawbone of an ass. His mighty strokes opened a bloody path through the press for survivors. They staggered out and back to blue-clad lines that still held.

With them rolled only two of their guns, one hauled by its team, the other by matrosses in a bricole and with dragropes. "Hancock" and "Adams" had been saved, but "Mistress Lucy" and "Frederick the Great" were missing—in the hands of the enemy.

As night fell, the American army quit the field. Its loss was alarmingly heavy: 300 killed, 600 wounded, and 400 prisoners. Fortunately unpursued, it retreated to Chester.

Andrews and his remaining men made their way to the artillery park. They waited there in sad silence, their thoughts on comrades who would never answer roll call again: Connors and the youngster who had died with him under the bayonets, both true to the end to the spirit of the artillery, along with the others who were gone. In utter dejection and weariness they hung their heads. They had lost two of their guns. Nor was it any comfort that they had plenty of company in the shame they felt. From other batteries another of the Hessian cannon, captured at Trenton had been taken and so had been nine others including a howitzer, five fine brass pieces sent from France, and one of American make, along with their teams and ammunition wagons. Since artillery first appeared on battlefields, captured guns had ever been a trophy of victory, guns lost a gage of defeat. The artillerymen, gathered in the park, tasted the bitter dregs of disgrace. Few could bear to look up when General Knox came striding among them.

Knox spoke, and at his words dull eyes brightened, and men held up their heads again.

"You stood to your guns even after our infantry supports were gone, even when you were surrounded by the enemy. And still you fought on.

"This day"—Knox's voice grew deeper with emotion—"this day my corps did me great honor."

There was no saving Philadelphia. The last barrier was broken when Wayne's brigade was surprised at Paoli. British General Grey, who that night won the name of "No-flint" by ordering flints taken from his men's muskets, thus forcing them to rely on the bayonet, swooped down at 2 A.M. Wayne was routed with heavy loss, though he managed to bring off his guns. Later he would redeem himself by storming Stony Point, New York, with the bayonet, but the lesson he had learned was costly in lives.

A few days later Howe and Cornwallis marched into Philadelphia, and British troops also occupied Germantown, five miles away. At the latter place Washington tried to turn the tide, launching a spirited attack that at first swept everything before it.

Andrews and his men, serving their old guns and two new ones drawn from the reserve, again fought with Sullivan's division. They marched with the cheering American advance that scarcely paused until it halted before Judge Chew's big stone house. Six companies of the British 40th Foot had garrisoned it, and their muskets spat fire from every window. They shot down an officer, sent to demand surrender.

Storm the house or by-pass it and march on? Washington turned for advice to the trusted Knox.

"Never leave a hedgehog in your rear, sir," Knox answered. Those were classical tactics, drawn from the best military treatises.

Washington nodded. "Open fire with your guns, General," he ordered.

The cannon ringed the house and thundered. Andrews watched in frustration as the balls from his three-pounders bounced off the stone walls like slugs from a pea-shooter. Six-pounders, the heaviest guns on hand, had no greater effect. The door and window frames were blown in, but the defenders kept up so hot a fire that no assault could be delivered. At last the command to march on, leaving a battalion to mount guard over the garrison in the stone house, was given. Andrews, limbering up his guns, saw a crestfallen look on Knox's face. For once the General's knowledge of warfare, learned from books, had misled him. Precious time and the impetus of the attack had been lost. All hope of victory was ended by stubborn British resistance and by a thick fog which threw American columns into confusion and caused them to fire on each other.

Germantown was defeat but no disaster. More than counteracting it, some weeks later came splendid news that General Burgoyne, invading from Canada with an army of Britons, Brunswickers, and Indians, had been roundly beaten and forced to surrender at Saratoga. General Gates had held the American command, but it was the dashing leadership of Benedict Arnold, along with Stark's at Bennington, that had won the victory.

Still Howe held Philadelphia, and there the British, secure and comfortable, settled down for the winter. Twenty miles away, Washington's army made camp on the bleak and snowy fields of Valley Forge.

Chapter XV

Cold Forge

THE woods around Valley Forge rang with the blows of axes. Sergeant Sampson, swinging his like the trail spike he had wielded at the Battle of Brandywine, urged on his squad as he worked. In the sharp December air, panting men breathed white steam.

"Take it easier, Sarge," Brooks begged. "You're going at it like these were British trees. Up home when I was a boy I remember tall pines, marked with the King's arrow. Meant they were reserved as masts for the Royal Navy. There's none of those around here."

"Close your trap and get busy," Sampson bellowed. "Want to sleep around a fire in the open again tonight? Besides, first hut built gets a prize from General Washington."

125

Brooks drove a wedge, splitting a log. "No use," he said. "Bunch of infantrymen over there got a headstart. One hut—twelve men, eh? That'll just hold our squad. Let's make ours a bit bigger and take a horse in to help keep us warm."

A driver laughed, then looked worried. "Wish we could. Poor critters! It'll go hard with 'em out in the open. Mebbe we can build a shed over 'em later."

Lieutenant Andrews, toiling alongside his men, spoke up. "Another reason to hurry is this. General Washington's living in a shabby tent. He won't move into quarters till we're under roofs."

Soldiers who were woodsmen and handy with tools made the cabins spring up, neatly arranged according to the General's plan. As each group finished its own shelter, it joined in erecting redoubts and entrenchments that would make the camp a strong fortress. Brooks looked up from the gun emplacement he was digging and called to his lieutenant.

"Sir," he said, "I guess this might be a right pleasant spot in the summer. But I don't think I'm going to like it at all in the winter."

Andrews smiled. "Nor I, Corporal, but this is where we have to be. From here we can keep watch on the British. We can make raids and cut off some of the food going into Philadelphia. And come spring, we'll be on hand to hit them again."

"Yes, sir. Sounds right military and even reasonable. But —you've read Shakespeare, sir?"

"Yes. Used to sell his plays in the shop in Boston."

"You know the court fool in *King Lear*, the one that's always saying, 'Poor Tom's a cold'? Well, something tells me that hereabouts poor Eph's going to be a-colder still."

It was cold even inside the huts where ragged men, swathed in blankets, huddled around small, smoky fires. How fortunate it was that they had finished those shelters before hunger began to sap their strength. Food was so scarce now that soldiers grew more feeble and irritable by the day. At first angry complaints that there was no meat ran through the encampment. Then all hope of an issue of even stringy beef disappeared, and there was nothing to eat but fire-cakes—lumps of dough baked on a hot stone—fire-cake and water, no more, for every meal.

Once Andrews saw Brooks and some of his gun squad gathered around an iron pot boiling over a campfire. He walked over, hoping to smell a nourishing stew or soup, but he sniffed in vain. There was nothing in the bubbling water but a large stone. Brooks managed a half-grin at his lieutenant's look of surprise and said:

"They say there's strength in a stone, if only you can get it out. Anyway, sir, the hot water will warm our innards."

More meagre still grew the rations, and the army came close to mutiny. Officers, making rounds of the huts to muster details for guard or fatigue, were defied by angry troopers who poked their heads outdoors and yelled, "No bread, no soldier!" Yet they did not long refuse duty when the officers, shivering, unmilitary figures shrouded in blankets or old dressing gowns, called out the guard. Men pooled their clothing so a sentry could be clad warmly enough to endure his freezing patrol. While the contributors, half-naked, crouched closer about their fire, the man for duty stumbled out, grumbling bitterly, took his place in ranks, and the guard shouldered muskets and marched off. Shoeless soldiers winced as knife-like ridges of frozen mud cut through the sacking around their feet, and crimson stains on the snow traced the route of the guard to the outposts.

In the southern part of camp, where Knox's guns were parked near Poor's and Wayne's brigades, the artillerymen were routed out to man fieldpieces in the fortified line for long, frigid vigils. Andrews, taking his tour of duty with his crews, never ceased to marvel at the privations men were willing to suffer for patriotism, for the ideal of freedom. Captain Nathan Hale, hanged as a spy by the British in New York, had died declaring his regret that he had but one life to give for his country. Here at Valley Forge soldiers were dying a slower and less appalling death than one by the gallows, but as surely giving their lives for the same cause—dying of camp fever, dysentery, and lung sickness, or becoming cripples when frostbitten legs had to be amputated. In spite of it all, desertions were not large.

As heartrending as the scenes in the crowded hospitals was the dumb agony of the artillery horses. The nearest farm where any feed could be obtained was eighteen miles away. Often weary foragers, scouring the countryside, could find none at all. Hundreds of the poor animals on the picket lines died and had to be buried in the winter-hardened ground with backbreaking labor. The survivors, mere bone-racks, somehow were kept alive. In sudden need they might be able to pull the guns into action.

Would the army last through this dreadful winter or must it be disbanded and the struggle for liberty lost? Andrews, in despair, went to see Henry Knox.

The Chief of Artillery, his natural buoyancy at a low ebb, spoke bitterly. "General Washington has repeatedly told the Congress that if it does not supply us, the army must inevitably perish of starvation, or disappear by wholesale desertion. Congress will not listen. It pays heed only to those jealous plotters, Generals Gates and Conway and their crowd, who are seeking to undermine our Commander and force his dismissal.

"Kent, you and I have read history. Black on its pages will stand the names of so-called statesmen of the Continental Congress who are letting us freeze and starve and die here!"

"The verdict of history will be too late to save us, sir. Of course the men don't blame General Washington. I've seen their eyes when they watch him ride around camp. There's devotion in them."

"I know. I've seen it, too. And he bears the heaviest burden of us all. Kent, tomorrow is his birthday. I wish I could parade all my corps and salute him with every cannon we have. He wouldn't permit it. The men are too cold and hungry for any extra effort. No, it would not. . . . Wait, I have it. Present my compliments to Colonel Proctor and ask him to report to me here."

Next day an event took place which Andrews remembered all his life—the first public celebration of Washington's birthday.

Drums rolled and fifes shrilled. Through the camp marched the band of Proctor's Fourth Continental Artillery, its tall drum-major marking the tempo with his staff. On the flanks the fife-major and the music master bent critical ears toward pupils who responded by doing them proud. Drummer boys, in their early teens or younger, joyfully beat flams and flourishes. Fifers, despite cold-cramped fingers and blue lips, missed hardly a trill of the "Old Continental March." Men came tumbling out of the

huts to form a column behind the band. How music could
lift hearts! A mob of skinny scarecrows suddenly became a
marching army, swinging along at the quickstep.

Yonder in the doorway of his quarters stood Washington, beside him his wife Martha who had recently come to
join him, her comely face beaming with a happy smile.
Behind the band, playing loudly and enthusiastically, the
ragamuffin soldiers crowded. Now the fifers struck up
"Yankee Doodle." Andrews heard Brooks beside him speak
softly:

"Sir, they'll never be singing the 'Captain Washington'
verse any more."

That was the verse somebody had made up when Washington first took command of the army at Cambridge, and
the rank and file distrusted the aristocratic planter from
Virginia, stern and austere on his charger in the midst of
his staff.

> And there was Captain Washington,
> And gentle folks about him.
> They say he's grown so tarnal proud
> He will not ride without 'em.

No, they'd never sing that verse—not these soldiers, here
to pay him homage on his birthday and show him their
faith and their love. If he was proud, it was pride in them.
For his sake—for the country for which he stood as gloriously as the starry banner flying from its staff there—they
would endure, they would see this bitter winter through.

Lucy Knox made the long and dangerous journey from
Massachusetts to Valley Forge. To be with her beloved
Henry, so friends said, she followed the army like a drum.
Energetically she joined Martha Washington and the wives

of Generals Greene and Stirling in helping to care for the sick. With their efforts and those of the kindly Moravians in their hospital at Bethlehem, the dismal lot of the invalids began to brighten.

Mistress Lucy greeted Andrews, summoned to the Knox quarters, with the affection of an old friend. "I brought a letter for you, Kent," she said, "but I doubt if you deserve it. Why Constancy has bothered to write you, I can't understand."

"Why not, ma'am? I've written her. Why shouldn't she answer?"

Lucy frowned. "Take off that air of injured innocence, young man. I'm going to give you a scolding, poorly though you look. Yes, you've written her once in a great while, but such letters! Oh, she hasn't confided in me, but I can well imagine there's little enough in those skimpy screeds of yours. I've seen her open them."

"We've been busy fighting a war."

"Yes, and she's proud of you. Henry wrote me about you at Trenton and the other battles, and I told Constancy. Never a word did she have from you about them."

"But how could I go bragging about . . ."

"Very well, Sir Modest. You couldn't. But when she wrote you of her pride in your gallant deeds, there was no need for your response being so much cold porridge."

"But I . . ."

"Oh, I know it's none of my affair. Call me an interfering busybody."

"Why, I'd never call . . ."

"No, you wouldn't. Not to my face. I am, though. But I simply can't bear having that lovely girl hurt. Now make no mistake, young man. She's not languishing for you. She has plenty of suitors among the stay-at-homes and others, no doubt. Would you like me to tell you what's bothering you, Kent?"

"Well, I'd . . ."

"I'll tell you anyway. It's that wounded British officer she nursed in Boston. Jealousy, sir, is lack of faith. Enough! I've said far more than I meant to. Come have dinner with us now. Very obviously you need it more than Henry does. Somehow he's kept flesh on his bones, as he did when you brought the guns from Fort Ti. Do you remember how that Doctor Byles at Cambridge looked at Henry and joked, 'I've never seen so fat an ox'?"

"A frightful pun, Mistress Lucy."

"Henry didn't think it was funny." Lucy rose and took Andrews' arm. "Neglectful though you are of womankind, I'm fond of you, Kent," she said. "Come, take me into dinner—what there is of it."

There began to be more food for the hungry army. General Wayne won the nickname of "The Drover" by leading a foraging expedition that brought in a herd of bullocks. General Greene took over the Quartermaster Generalcy, and under the management of that able officer supplies came in slowly but steadily. Gaunt frames filled out, and spring came back into steps.

Then arrived a Prussian veteran, sent over by wise old Ben Franklin, American Ambassador to France—Baron Friedrich Wilhelm August Heinrich Ferdinand von Steuben, to give him his full, his very full, name. Washington appointed him Inspector General, recognizing him as a master drillmaster, and gave him free rein to make the army over. Grinning artillerymen watched him take the infantry in hand, yelling commands in broken English, French, and German. He marched columns around camp, chanting, "Vun, two, tree, four," until an American officer gruffly complained, "This is sergeants' work," "I vas a sergeant meinself alretty," von Steuben retorted, and marched the officer along with his troops.

Andrews marveled at the musketry drill the German veteran conducted. *Poise firelock. Handle cartridge. Prime. Shut pan. Charge with cartridge. Draw rammer. Ram down cartridge. Return rammer.* It was nearly as complicated as firing a cannon, and von Steuben insisted on the same precision and speed Knox demanded of his artillery. Such disciplined fire, along with practiced maneuvers on the battlefield, and the bayonet fighting the Baron was also teaching, could mean the difference between defeat and victory.

Not for long were the artillerymen allowed to be amused spectators on the sidelines. Von Steuben let his infantrymen rest while he roared at the men around the guns, "Und you, ver you vas ven die infantry she march? Die cannon mit die brigades alvays must go." He ordered them to man dragropes and join the marching column with their guns, to the vast delight of the foot troops. Discovering that Andrews spoke French, the Baron made him interpret lectures on the duties of lieutenants and non-commissioned officers and help aides translate drill regulations.

The warmth of spring completed the revival of the army that had so nearly wasted away from starvation and cold. There was energy and spirit to spare now for duties and even for sports. Officers played cricket, but the enlisted men preferred a game, recently introduced from England, called rounders or base-ball. Shad began to run in the Schuylkill River, and soldier-fishermen netted hundreds which became thousands when cooperating cavalrymen charged into the shallows and drove masses of the shining fish into the nets. In the evening delicious aromas rose from the cook-fires where the army feasted royally on shad and roe.

Von Steuben's training proved its worth when General Lafayette led a foray of two thousand men to test the strength of the enemy outposts. The British, informed by a deserter, mustered twice that number and marched stealthily out of Philadelphia, confident of capturing "the Boy," as they called the young French marquis, and sending him back as a trophy to England. They struck the American encampment on Barren Hill at dawn, but this time there was no panic, no rout. After the first shock, the Americans rallied and coolly beat back every attack. The jaws of the trap closed on empty trenches, as Lafayette calmly withdrew his men and guns, his losses light and fewer than the Britishers'. Chagrined, the Redcoat columns hurriedly retreated when Washington rushed to the rescue with his whole force.

Now came the most splendid news since the Declaration of Independence. France had allied herself with the United States against her hereditary foe, and was dispatching a fleet, an army, and supplies across the Atlantic. Wild rejoicing filled Valley Forge, so short a time ago a place of despair. Chaplains preaching sermons of thanksgiving were cut off promptly after half an hour by a cannon shot. Gunner Brooks, detailed to that duty, performed it enthusiastically and insisted that after the war he was going to introduce the custom to curb long-winded preachers in Boston.

A grand review was ordered, and the brigades marched smartly to the parade ground where they formed in line, two of the wings commanded by foreign officers serving the American cause: Lafayette and de Kalb. With Andrews at his gun stood a young French artilleryman, Chevalier de Tousard, who had fought gallantly at Brandywine and Germantown. The artillery boomed out a thirteen-gun salute, followed by a running fire of musketry that rippled from man to man along the lines and by loud huzzas for the King of France and the American States. Proudly von Steuben listened to the precision of the *feu de joie*—the joyful firing—fruit of his labors.

In Philadelphia news of the French alliance spread consternation through the British garrison. No longer could command of the seas be counted upon, with a French fleet already on it way across the ocean and the young American navy also to be reckoned with, for John Paul Jones had even dared raid the coast of England. General Clinton, Howe's successor, could not risk being penned up in Philadelphia, cut off from New York and the only other British Army in America. He gave orders to evacuate and march north. The columns with their long wagon train moved out of Philadelphia and scarcely had they quit the town when Light-horse Harry Lee and his cavalrymen galloped in to speed their departure.

Farewell to Valley Forge. Break camp. Washington mustered his army for pursuit. Kent Andrews hurried to the Knox quarters to bid good-by to Mistress Lucy, sad at having to leave her Henry again. He handed her two fat letters and begged her to deliver them in Boston.

Lucy smiled. "They're not both to your mother, I see," she said. "It seems my tongue doesn't run altogether in vain."

Andrews grinned back at her. "I had to tell Constancy how staunchly the men endured last winter here. She'll be glad to know. She's a patriot. I haven't forgotten how she warned us that night in Boston when the British tried to seize our guns."

"High time your memory was jogged, young man. I'll fill in what you left out. I misdoubt you said much of yourself."

"Oh, I put in an 'I' here and there."

He did not mention a final sentence he had been unable to refrain from writing: "At the Battle of Brandywine I think we came up against the Royal Welch Fusiliers. I could not be sure I recognized their uniform. We lost two guns and had to get out in a hurry. But I daresay you will welcome even vague news of the Royal Welch—if you have not had it from another source—because of your natural interest in an officer of that regiment."

Lucy Knox looked at him shrewdly. "There's nothing you'd like to add to your letters—or change?" she asked. It was disturbing how the woman could read a man's mind. Andrews hesitated, then stubbornly shook his head.

Drums were beating "The General," signal to form and march. On impulse Andrews followed the graceful custom he had learned from French officer friends. He bent and kissed Lucy's hand.

"I'll pass that on, Kent," she promised, as he hastened off to his guns.

CHAPTER XVI

Heat of Combat

AS THE American army eagerly pushed northward on the trail of the retreating British, Kent Andrews surveyed the long column of which his guns and ammunition carts, bumping along behind their teams, formed a part. It stretched out for miles, with cavalry scouting far ahead. Batteries of two or more guns rolled in the midst of brigades they supported. Close behind Andrews' three-pounders marched a company of Pennsylvania infantry. Glancing over his shoulder, he saw a woman, trudging beside a soldier on the left flank of the leading squad, and farther back he caught sight of a few other skirts fluttering beside the blue-and-brown-clad ranks.

Women, who stayed with their men in camp and on the march and waited at the edges of battlefields, were not unusual in the army, nor were they unwelcome. Enduring hard campaigning without complaint, they made them-

137

selves highly useful as nurses, cooks, and laundresses. Andrews smiled to himself at the thought that Lucy would probably be riding beside Henry Knox now if he had permitted it. Members of Andrews' gun crew would have been as sternly denied feminine company by him, though there was an artillery tradition behind it. He remembered reading that in early European wars companies of the Gunners' Guild were often family affairs, and that boys born in camp were called "sons of guns."

Andrews saw that the woman back there was shyly beckoning to him. He dropped back to the head of the infantry column.

It was the soldier on the flank who spoke first. "Private Hays, Pennsylvania Line, sir," he said. "This is my wife, Molly. She wanted a word with you if you don't mind."

Molly's ruddy, homely face, plainly Pennsylvania Dutch, was beaming as she said, "Had to tell you, Lieutenant, that it's good to be close to the artillery. Johnny and me, we used to be with the guns."

"First Pennsylvania Artillery," Hays added.

"Can't see why you ever left us for the infantry." Andrews answered, grinning.

"Johnny's time was up, and we went home for a while," Molly explained. "When he re-enlisted, there wasn't any artillery handy, so we joined up here. I kind of miss the guns and especially the horses. I was a farm girl."

"I've an idea we lost a good matross and a good artillery woman," Andrews said.

"You did at that, sir," Hays put in. "Molly learned gun drill from watching me at it."

"All the same, Hays, keep her out of range if we get in a fight," Andrews urged before he strode ahead to overtake his gun.

Hays called after him, "I'll try to, sir, but 't ain't easy."

Andrews saluted General Knox, riding past on the left of a tall, surly-faced major-general, with Alexander Hamilton, now a lieutenant-colonel and Washington's aide, trotting behind them. They must be bound for a council of war, Andrews guessed. Hamilton, seeing his friend, pulled his horse down to a walk.

"I envy you," the New Yorker said. "Give me the guns rather than the staff any day, especially with action ahead."

"We will attack, won't we?" Andrews asked.

"If I know General Washington, we will." Hamilton leaned down from his saddle and spoke softly. "But I'll make you a wager. That old sour phiz you saw riding by with our admirable artillery Brigadier will oppose an attack. Did you recognize him? That's General Charles Lee, once of His Brittanic Majesty's Army and a veteran of long service. Turned his coat and came over to us. Last year British dragoons caught him asleep and took him prisoner. Unhappily he was exchanged and is back on our hands. I don't think General Washington trusts him much, though he defers to Lee's military record. Certainly I wouldn't assign the fellow command of a corporal's guard. Well, *au revoir*, Kent, as we French scholars say. Give the Redcoats a round shot for me."

Sunday, June 28th, 1778, dawned hot and gave promise of growing torrid. Veterans drank sparingly from their canteens, refilling them at streams where artillery drivers watered their thirsty teams. Ammunition wagons were heavier from the weight of extra water jugs; the sloshing buckets, slung beneath the gun-carriages, would soon run dry on a day like this. Already the burning sun had heated gun barrels so that they were almost too hot to touch; they would have to be swabbed cool even before the first powder charge was rammed down to the breech. Sweating soldiers scowled ruefully at the memory of the Valley Forge winter when they had sworn that no weather would ever be too warm for them again. Coats were unbuttoned or shed and carried, and it was mostly a shirt-sleeved army that pressed after the British rear guard, sweltering in heavy uniforms and under full pack.

Musketry crackled up ahead in the direction of Monmouth Court House, near the town of Freehold, New Jersey. Andrews nodded with satisfaction at the opening of the fight, but watched General Charles Lee ride by with misgivings. Lee, as Hamilton had foretold, had opposed an attack and declined command of the vanguards; then shifted and wheedled it from Lafayette, with Washington reluctantly acquiescing. Andrews, marking Lee's dour and lowering look, thought: that man has no confidence either in the Commander-in-Chief or in us, the men he's leading. We'll have to win this battle in spite of him.

Now Lafayette's and Wayne's brigades were engaged, pressing in on Clinton's rear guard, strengthened with his best British regiments which had faced about and deployed to meet the American assault. Andrews' gun chimed into the cannonade which boomed above the infantry volleys. Its three-pound balls were no bigger than apples, but their effect was deadly when they plowed into the close-packed British ranks. Front and rear files toppled, and the iron spheres hurtled on, to smash into companies in support. When the guns moved up, closing the range, loaders would shift to grapeshot whose spray of pellets, about the size of musket balls, would do deadlier work still.

Never had Andrews seen the infantry deliver such steady, rapid fire. The sun gleamed on bayonets fixed for a charge.

But no word to charge was given. Instead, poised lines incredulously heard shouts of "Fall back, fall back!" as a staff officer galloped up with orders from General Lee. Lafayette and Mad Anthony Wayne raged when their men were jerked back from the brink of victory, but they obeyed and drew off their brigades. There was no disorder, never a hint of panic, in the retreat. Rear-guard companies halted and checked the foe, then sullenly gave ground again. Artillery, unlimbering to fire a round, limbered again and merged with the ebbing tide.

Through the din of battle thundered the beat of pound-ing hoofs. Warned by Hamilton, General Washington on a big chestnut charger burst onto the field at a headlong gallop. Andrews had witnessed that same superb sight at Princeton. He watched the Commander rein up in front of Charles Lee. What took place between them was as plain to spectators as if they had heard every word. Washington sternly demanding an explanation for the retreat, Lee, a picture of miserable confusion, stammering and stuttering; the furious scorn of the great Virginian's reprimand, and Lee quailing and cringing beneath it.

Now Washington was seen to fling his arm around in a terrible gesture toward the rear. Charles Lee, head sunk on his chest, rode away on the dark path that led to court-martial and suspension from the army in disgrace, though he would escape the full penalty of his perfidy. Not until after his lonely, embittered death, years later, would it be known that the double turncoat, while a British prisoner, had given Howe a plan for conquering America.

Washington's rallying took the retreating brigades,

cheering, back into battle. Knox galloped up and placed a mixed battalion of artillery on a hill, where Andrews' guns and others poured round after round of grapeshot into the oncoming British, paving the way for gallantly assaulting American infantry. As von Steuben's bayonet men dashed in with a whoop, the smoking guns fell silent.

Andrews, suddenly weak, tottered over to clutch a wheel of one of his three-pounders to keep himself from falling. The temperature was in the nineties now and soaring close to one hundred degrees. How much longer could men fight on through such scorching heat? Andrews, not far from fainting, saw that Brooks was slumped over the trail of the piece, and every matross in the crew lay gasping on the ground. Only big Sergeant Sampson was still on his feet, staggering up with an armful of cannon balls from the ammunition chest.

Andrews heard a woman's voice behind him, "Here, Lieutenant." The girl Molly he had met back on the march was holding out a pitcher of water. With a moan, he reached eagerly for it, then dragged his hand back and made her give his men drinks before he took a blessed, reviving draft. He turned to the girl and said:

"With all our hearts thanks, Mistress Molly—I can't remember your last name."

"Never mind," she answered. "The boys have been calling me Molly Pitcher all day. I'll get more water. Four or five of your men still can't get up. You'll need them when you open fire again."

The officer bent over his prostrate matrosses. Several, sun-struck, were completely out of action. "Molly," he called after her, "can you bring your artilleryman husband? I need him badly."

"Certain, sir. He'll come gladly, and our Cap'n'll spare him."

She ran off toward the infantry, paying no heed to humming bullets. Soon she was back, Hays at her side. The former artilleryman dropped his musket, picked up a rammer staff and took his post.

Again the guns on the hill roared into action, opening on the Royal Artillery which had moved up and engaged them in a crashing, flaming duel. Spurred on by General Knox, who had taken direct command, the American cannonade swelled into a violent crescendo. But the enemy's fire rose in volume and fury to match it. Andrews saw a cannon ball shear off the head of a captain directing the fire of a gun to his right. Hardly had he turned, shaken, back to his own gun, when a shell burst close by. Hays cried out and sank down, clutching a wound in his shoulder.

Every man of the reduced crew had been doing double duty, with the lieutenant himself serving as second gunner. Rate of fire would be badly slowed now that a good loader had been put out of action. Even Sergeant Sampson was swaying on his feet. Well, they must keep firing somehow. The officer, about to give an order, blinked sweat-blurred eyes. A striped skirt flashed in front of him, as Molly Pitcher bent over her fallen husband, grabbed up the staff and rushed to the gun muzzle.

Automatically Andrews croaked orders. "Sponge piece." Molly cooled the hot bore. Expertly she reversed the staff and was ready for the command, "Ram down cartridge." She thrust the powder charge down to the breach and stepped smartly back clear of the wheels. "Prime. Take aim. Fire!" The gun slammed, recoiled. Sturdy Molly ran to help shove it back into battery. For her gallant services she would win a warrant as sergeant from General Washington.

Over there the enemy guns had had enough and were pulling out. But now from the right marched lines of scarlet-coated guards and light infantry—and of blue-clad Hessian grenadiers, advancing to the assault. American infantry, changing front, caught them in a deadly crossfire, and at the same moment Knox's cannon shifted aim to enfilade the ranks of the attackers. Brooks jumped up and yelled as the gun he had sighted fired. Its ball had smashed muskets from the hands of a whole British platoon. Shattered, the assault reeled back in headlong retreat over fields littered with dead, wounded, and sun-struck men.

Drive them; smash the rest of Sir Henry Clinton's army! His troops were too exhausted to march on this evening and make their escape. Yet the Americans were as far gone in utter weariness as their foe. As the merciless sun sank below the horizon, infantrymen dropped in their tracks and slept. Around every gun its crew lay inert.

Andrews woke in the middle of the night. Some of his matrosses were begging pitifully for water. He dragged himself up and fetched a bucket. Before him gaped a ravine with a marshy bottom where a stream probably ran. As he started off, he sensed someone beside him, and heard Brooks' voice saying, "I'll go with you, sir. We'll be needing a couple of bucketsful." Andrews patted the gunner's shoulder affectionately. It was good to have a man you could always count on, who never failed you.

They groped their way down into the ravine over a causeway that sloped into it, a passage Andrews had noticed before nightfall. Here, he thought, was a route the guns could use when the British were pursued tomorrow.

Day must dawn soon now. There was a faint glimmering in the eastern sky.

Deep in the ravine they heard the rippling of water, and hurried on. Yes, here flowed a cool stream, and the two plunged their faces in it and drank long and thirstily before filling their buckets, unaware of the tread of booted feet behind them.

Sharp pricks of saber points in their backs. Hands jerking them up roughly. A Cockney voice grating, "Rebels, ain't ye? Figgered first ye was 'orses. Ye drank more'n ourn did. Hands behind ye quick, if you don't want a blade through your guts. Tie 'em up, lads, and a couple of ye run the cords to your saddle rings.

"Mount hup." Leather creaked and hoofs stamped. Andrews and Brooks, tugged along, heard the harsh voice again. "Sorry, we can't let you wait and say good-by to Gen'rul Washington. Anyhow 'e won't be awake. Getting 'is beauty sleep, 'e is. H'it's bound for New York ye are with the Light Dragoons. March, ye lousy Rebels, march!"

CHAPTER XVII

Prisoners of War

T HE hopes of the two captured artillerymen sank lower with each mile they trudged north in a closely guarded column of prisoners. Vainly they strained their ears for the sound of a fusilade from the rear, as a signal that Washington's army was overtaking the retreating British. No shots broke the calm of the morning. Chances of an attack that might mean rescue dwindled and vanished.

Under the threat of guards' bayonets, the prisoners shuffled on through choking dust. It was humiliating to be captured, Andrews reflected morosely, even though you surrendered with a saber point at your back. When he and Brooks were missed, Sergeant Sampson must have followed the path down into the ravine, spotted the abandoned buckets and the hoofprints of the dragoon horses and guessed their fate. The big non-com probably had

146

gone straight to General Knox himself to report their capture. That same thought had struck Brooks whose dust-caked lips were curved in a grin.

"I can see the good old Sarge when he found out we'd been rounded up," the gunner said. "I play plenty of jokes on him, but I'm fond of that great hulk. I'll wager he went straight to Headquarters, ranting and roaring, 'Turn out the guard! Turn out the whole army! The Lobsters have their claws on the best artillery lieutenant and the best gunner corporal you've got, General Knox, and if you don't go pry 'em loose, I will.'"

Andrews had to smile. "I wouldn't put it far past him," he answered, then lapsed back into his melancholy. "Might as well acknowledge we're snagged," he said. "Fortunes of war. We'll have to wait our chance to break loose."

"Not a chance of it, sir, until after we're cooped up back in New York. Then as an officer you can apply to be exchanged."

Andrews considered and came to a sudden decision. "No. I won't ask for that. My coat and hat are back by the gun. There's nothing on me to show my rank. I'll not claim it."

"You've got to, sir. It's your duty, Lieutenant."

"Make it Kent. No title and no 'sirs' from now on. That's an order, Eph."

"But, sir . . ."

"Hush! You heard what I said."

"But, s—, I mean K-Kent—you've no reason to —I mean it's much tougher in prison on soldiers than officers. There's no sense in letting yourself in for that when you don't have to."

"Isn't there? I think there is. What would you do in my place? Let me go, and take it alone?"

"That's no argument. I'm a gunner corporal—a good one maybe—but you're an experienced lieutenant of artillery and due for a captaincy, if you ask me. Tote up the values. There's no question but . . ."

"Cease firing, Eph. My mind's made up. You followed me down into that ravine, didn't you? I'm sticking with you now. As for exchange, that's slow and doubtful for junior officers. I'm not going to wait for it. Working together, you and I might be able to escape. That's how it's going to be."

Brooks saw the determination on his companion's face and sighed with resignation. Then he said with a chuckle, "I'm going to have a time minding my tongue and forgetting those 'sirs.' It's got to be a habit. Say, how would it do if I made it 'Sir Kent'? With this chivalrous notion of yours, you're carrying on like all those knights of old I've read about."

Andrews smiled. It would take a grim prison indeed to down the gay spirits of this friend of his.

Long marching brought the prisoners, footsore and dirty to the Hudson River. Ferried over to New York, they were herded, limping, through the town and halted at the Sugar House on Liberty Street.

In that gloomy, gray stone building there had been no sugar since the first hungry American prisoners from Fort Washington had scraped dregs from the bottoms of its vats. It was surrounded by a nine-foot fence, so alertly patrolled by British and Hessian sentries that Liberty Street had become a travesty on its name. White faces, crowded close together, peered from narrow windows. Every ten minutes a new lot replaced them at the barred openings; relays, as the newcomers would soon learn, were taking turns to catch a breath of fresh air.

Andrews and Brooks, recognizing the prison from appalling tales of it that had filtered back to the American army, looked at each other and shuddered. As a chamber of horrors, the Sugar House vied with the Provost Jail and the black, suffocating holds of the prison ships in the harbor, known as "floating hells." Here reigned cruelty, starvation, and disease. These thick walls pent up the scorching summer heat and the bitterest cold of winter. There was said to be no escape but death from this confinement. Such was the evil fame of the place that the newly arrived prisoners shrank from entering. Guards shoved them roughly through the gates with musket butts and lined them up in a rocking corridor.

"Welcome, me honored guests!" A coarse-faced man, with brutality marked on every feature, grinned malevolently at them. "I'm your host, Sergeant O'Keefe—you've heard of me mebbe—bidding you take your ease in my inn. It's sorry I am that Provost Marshal Cunningham's not here to greet you. But he'll soon be back with the fleet from Philadelphia where he ran the prison to the King's taste. Had the Rebels eating the mortar and wood and clay off the walls of their cells there, he did. Belike he'll try that fare here. That did the trick, and it's overcrowded we are, too. The Provost Marshal swears he's killed off more Rebels than all His Majesty's armies, and yon's no idle boast, me hearties."

Andrews felt Brooks tug at his arm and heard him whisper, "Please, sir, I beg of you, tell him you're an officer. Before it's too late. You'll never come out of here alive."

The lieutenant shook his head and gripped the gunner's arm hard to silence him.

O'Keefe was glaring at them. "Pipe down there! Jailers, lock these cursed Rebels up."

Weeks dragged interminably into months. The two artillerymen, vainly exploring every means of escape they could
think of, found only one, O'Keefe's repeated offer: "Fifty
guineas bounty to enlist in His Majesty's service." Should
they join a Tory regiment and wait their chance to desert?
No, too many stories had come back through the prison
grapevine of men who had tried it and been forced to
fight against their comrades. If they refused, they were
shot or hanged on the spot. Andrews and Brooks sank into
the lethargy of prison routine, and soon it took all their
strength and efforts to keep alive on the rations issued after
jailers had sold a good portion of them to line their pock-
ets. The rations were usually no more than mouldy, wormy
bread and filthy water, with sometimes a little rice and
peas and a rare piece of raw pork.

Once Andrews saw the cruel Cunningham kick over a
prisoner's soup kettle in a fit of temper. When the man
dared shout a protest, he was slashed viciously across the
face by the Provost Marshal's rattan cane. When Brooks
ran to his aid, O'Keefe beat the gunner over the head with
a heavy jail key, knocking him senseless. Later the culprits
were dragged to the whipping posts and given twenty
merciless lashes apiece. That night they lay face downward in the verminous straw on their cell floor, groaning
from the pain in their lacerated backs.

Jail fever, the flux, and smallpox took heavy toll in the
Sugar House. American doctors, sometimes admitted to
treat their countrymen, were unable to save many of the
wasted, feeble men. Andrews and Brooks, who miracu-
lously stayed free of diseases, would pull themselves to
their feet many a morning at the shout, "Rebels, bring out
your dead!" and carry the cold bodies of cell-mates down
to the waiting carts. Surely it would be only a question

of time before their own corpses were thrown into un-marked, mass graves on the outskirts of the city. Scarce a day passed without O'Keefe maliciously mocking them at morning roll call, "What, you two still alive? Musta been born to hang, and meself will be glad to oblige you."

A little while longer without hope, and O'Keefe might not have the trouble—or the pleasure—of hanging them. Men can die of despair. Andrews realized that they must make some attempt to escape, however desperate.

After considering various possibilities, none really prom-ising, he and Brooks decided to try to tunnel out from the cellar of the Sugar House, digging under its foundations. They chose a certain dark corner. If they succeeded in digging through from that point, they calculated, after a survey from the windows, that their escape opening would emerge under an abandoned, tumble-down shack which would screen them from patrolling sentries.

The three prisoners who spread their pallets in that corner must be taken into their plot. One was an infantry-man, another a dragoon, and the third a sailor. Other cellar prisoners would of course know what they were doing, but they would be sworn to secrecy and offered the chance to use the tunnel after the first escapees were in the clear.

Quickly the infantryman and dragoon agreed to join in the attempt. The sailor, whose right arm hung stiff at his side, firmly refused.

"Not for me," he said with finality. "For one thing, there's this crippled wing of mine. How I got it is the other reason."

As they huddled in the darkness, he told them his grim story.

"Happened on a prison ship where I was 'fore they sent me here," he related. "Tried the same thing you're figuring on, we did. We cut a hole through the hull in the gun room. Careful as could be, we was. Seemed nobody'd caught on to what we was up to.

"Opened up the hole one night and looked through. Too much moon, but that couldn't be helped. The shore yonder sure looked good. Not too much of a swim even for weak, half-starved men like we was. We swarmed down a rope— 'bout twenty of us—and struck out for shore.

"I'll make the rest of it short—like it was. The Britishers knew what we was doing all along. Boatload of 'em was waiting in the shadows off the starboard quarter. They follered our wakes, marked by the moonlight, as we swum. Then they opened up with their muskets. Picked up a few of us they missed. When I grabbed the gunwales as they was 'bout to run me down, one of 'em sliced me deep on the arm with a cutlass.

"So Jack here is through with escapes. Mebbe they sent me here to kinda discourage you lads. Well, if you gotta try, I'll keep it dark. But me now, I'm staying put."

Still they must try, Andrews, Brooks, and the others agreed. They started digging with a spike, sharp sticks, and a scraper. Dirt was stuffed inside their shirts, and they carried and hid it in another part of the Sugar House where it would not betray them. Every night the tunnel, large enough for only one crawling body, was driven forward a few yards. Then they began to slant it upward. It was grueling work for men half-ill, always hungry and steadily weakening. Determined spirit kept them at it, and hope lent them strength.

All the other cellar prisoners, their mounting enthusiasm barely concealed from the guards, helped where they could. Only one held himself aloof. He was a young man named Knowles, who claimed he had been a midshipman on a Boston frigate. He insisted that he should have been confined in an officers' prison instead of being shut up in the Sugar House with a lot of riffraff from the forecastle and the ranks. No attention was paid to his complaints. Knowles, a handsome fellow except for small, shifty eyes and overfull lips, had finally relapsed into sullen silence.

At last the diggers, worming in and out of the tunnel, estimated that they were within a few feet of breaking out. The next night, they told themselves elatedly, they would put their great venture to the trial.

In the darkness they gathered at the tunnel's mouth and shook hands. Brooks was to crawl through first, Andrews to be the rearmost. Fellow prisoners would close the aperture after them until they themselves were ready to use the avenue of escape a few days later. Brooks bent to enter.

Grate of key in lock. Screech of a heavy door on rusty hinges. Gleam of lanterns on musket barrels. A roar from the sergeant of the guard: "Come out o' there, you Rebel rats!"

Andrews, hustled off with the other three to be put in irons, saw the evilly triumphant grin on the face of Knowles. It was he, undoubtedly, who had betrayed them. Andrews, his thoughts desolate, telling himself again and again that he should have suspected, was roughly dragged away with the rest.

They were whipped again, merciless lashes on the scarcely healed scars of their first beating. Never removed were their heavy irons, linked by a chain. Andrews' irons, especially tight, tortured him. His wrists swelled under them until he could scarcely bear the pain. At length he appealed for relief, and one of the jailers, kinder than most, substituted a wider pair of manacles.

As hard to endure as the old irons were goading taunts by Knowles. Several times a day he would walk up to Andrews and take delight in baiting a man whose arms were chained and who could not retaliate.

"Want to run away again?" he would ask with a sneer. "When are you going home, soldier?"

The moment came when Andrews knew he had taken all he could. Tugging against his chain, he found he could slip his right wrist, the swelling gone down, from its iron. He waited till Knowles came close, freed his right arm, and smashed a fist with all his strength against the traitor's full-lipped mouth. Knowles screamed and toppled over, spitting out three teeth.

Prisoners cheering his downfall brought the guard. Meanwhile Andrews had slipped his wrist back into the iron. The men of the guard, with whom Knowles was no more popular than with his fellow prisoners, laughed off his assertion that Andrews had freed himself to strike him. Must have done it with irons on, the guard said, and more power to him.

Occasionally General Washington's commissioners, sent through the lines under a flag of truce to protest inhuman conditions in the prisons, succeeded in persuading the British commander to take some action. It was during one of those temporary reforms that the authorities decided to ship a number of prisoners out of New York.

Andrews and Brooks were on the list, perhaps because of their attempt to escape. Yet their names would have been cancelled from the list, they knew, if Jailer O'Keefe had not happened to be absent for a time on leave from the Sugar House. The artillerymen, hardly daring to believe their eyes, found themselves being pushed with a group through the gate they had expected only death or the end of the war would open for them. Guards marched them to the docks and aboard a transport.

"Where are we bound?" Andrews asked a sailor at the gangplank.

The tar, pity in his eyes as he stared at the prisoner's pale, peaked face and the gaunt frame in filthy rags, answered: "Halifax, mate. 'T ain't so bad in the clink up there, I hears. Anyhow can't be worse than where ye come from."

With more food and the sea air, the health and spirits of the prisoners began to revive. Off the Massachusetts coast Andrews gazed toward the fog-hidden shore with longing thoughts of home, his mother, and Constancy. Would he ever see them again? How desperately worried about him they must be. He had never been allowed to write from the Sugar House. Unless the American commissioner had managed to obtain a list of prisoners, they would not know whether he was alive or dead. Somewhere farther north had occurred the capture of the brigantine carrying Constancy to Halifax. Oh, for the sight of sails of American privateers, swooping in to the rescue! But that was a faint hope; the transport was too strongly convoyed by warships. Escape would have to wait until they reached Canada.

It must wait still longer. Andrews, Brooks, and some of their fellow prisoners never set foot on shore. In Halifax harbor they were put aboard a frigate which immediately set sail for England.

Brooks' grin broke through their gloom. "Sir Kent," he said, "once I bought a sheet of those Mother Goose rhymes you sold at the book shop, to read to my little sister. One of 'em comes back to me now." He struck an attitude and recited:

> Pussycat, pussycat, where have you been?
> I've been to London to look at the Queen.
> Pussycat, pussycat, what did you there?
> I frightened a little mouse under the chair.

"Well, now we're off to England, we might as well look the Queen over and while we're about it, we'll frighten old King George under his throne."

Andrews was too downcast to respond. All hope of freedom seemed ended now. English prisons were reported to be not a great deal better than the New York ones, although humane Englishmen had forced some improvement. Still a man must not give up.

"All right, Eph. We'll watch our chances to get away once we're ashore."

But they were not destined to land in England. Ordered into small boats, they were rowed across Liverpool harbor to a towering merchantman whose many gunports showed she was heavily armed.

Andrews, a question in his eyes, turned from the vessel they were approaching to a marine sergeant who had been kind to them during the voyage across the Atlantic.

"Hard lines," the sergeant muttered. "You're for it. That's an East Indiaman. It's off for India, Africa, or the spice islands you're bound. The John Company's bought you as slaves to work on its plantations."

In angry disbelief Andrews stared at him. "The John Company—the East India Company! You say we're sold to it as *slaves*? No! Your army can't do that! We're prisoners of war. Why—"

The marine broke in. "Well, they mayn't call you slaves, but from all I hear tell, it 'mounts to that. You're labor in safekeeping, taken off our army's hands. Prisoners of war got to work, don't they? That is, 'cepting the officers."

Andrews heard sputtering from the thwart beside him. He kicked Brooks violently on the shin. The gunner, in spite of orders, was surely about to reveal that his companion was an officer to save him from slavery. A glare reinforced the kick, and Brooks kept still.

The marine sergeant talked on, keeping his voice low. "You're right, 't is no way to be treatin' prisoners of war— no way to treat brave men. I fought your people at Lexington and Concord. Stout lads. Stood up to us and gave us a licking. We were lucky to make it back to Boston.

"Well, no help for it. Chin up and never say die."

When the prisoners climbed over the side, they were shackled and confined to the hold. The East India Company was taking no risk of losing property, bought and paid for. Below in the gloom, lit by the fitful gleam of a single lantern, the silence of despair prevailed. Men, doomed to slavery on the other side of the world, could not trust voices that might break.

How could they help abandoning all hope? Surely the last faint chance of ever seeing home again had vanished. Andrews and Brooks had known they would have been reported missing the day after the Battle of Monmouth and that it would be assumed that they had been captured. Surely General Knox would have made persistent efforts to find out where they were held as prisoners of war—to get word to them—to try to arrange an exchange. There was always a chance while they were in the Sugar House. Later, if they had been kept in prisons in Canada or England, their names must finally have appeared on a list.

Family and friends would learn they were alive, and the end of the war would see their release.

But now in the black hold of the East Indiaman, bound for the spice islands, Kent Andrews and Ephraim Brooks were convinced that their destiny was to disappear forever, without a trace.

Henry Knox had indeed striven mightily to locate his missing artillerymen. He had lost more than an able lieutenant and corporal—old friends, comrades from the beginning in the Boston artillery train. Alexander Hamilton, close to Washington as Knox was, also did all he could through Headquarters. Months passed without a glimmer of success. One stumbling block had been Andrews' refusal when taken prisoner to admit that he was an officer; the British truthfully answered inquiries saying that there was no Lieutenant Kent Andrews in any of their officers' prison camps. Were they holding a gunner named Brooks? The reply to that was that His Majesty's commanders were fighting a war and could not concern themselves with a search for some Rebel enlisted man rotting among the many in the hulks and cells.

At last Knox, Hamilton, and other friends acknowledged that there was nothing more they could do. Though still hoping against hope, they felt certain that Andrews and Brooks had been shot when they were captured or had died in prison, like so many others. Their memory as brave men would always be cherished. The cause in which they had sacrificed their lives must be won.

The fortunes of war rose and fell. From a bright promise, an alliance with France, money and arms came to the Americans; but still no French troops were landed who might turn the scale. The British won the next round by taking Savannah in South Carolina. Then in 1779, Mad

Anthony Wayne stormed the important British works at Stony Point, New York. A little American fleet under John Paul Jones was winning sea battles from the mighty British navy. But 1780 brought the shocking treason of General Benedict Arnold who nearly succeeded in betraying West Point and the control of the Hudson River to the enemy.

Back and forth tilted the balance. Sir Henry Clinton still firmly held New York City, and Washington's small army could do no more than watch and wait. The seat of war shifted south where a British fleet and army had captured Charleston, South Carolina, bagging General Lincoln and 5,000 men. Cornwallis, checked only temporarily by American victories at King's Mountain and Cowpens, marched on to ravage Georgia and the Carolinas, driving General Greene's force before him. If Greene were beaten, as seemed likely, British armies from the north and south would combine to crush Washington. The picture grew dark and gloomy.

Then dawned that glorious day in 1781 when a French fleet landed 4,000 elite troops at Newport, Rhode Island. Their commander, Count de Rochambeau, had orders to place his army at the disposal of General Washington. Furthermore, there was a second French fleet under Admiral De Grasse in the West Indies, ready to strike a doughty blow for American independence.

Washington detached a few thousand men to keep Clinton shut up in New York. Then he prepared to march south with the main body through New Jersey. There he was joined by Rochambeau and his veteran regiments, gallant in white uniforms with bright-colored facings. With high hopes the two forces, in parallel columns, hastened southward to crush Cornwallis.

Late one afternoon, when the armies had halted for the night, General Knox's tent was pitched near the artillery park. His orderly hung a mirror of burnished metal from a nail in the tent pole, and Knox began to shave. Suddenly he dropped his razor. His ruddy cheeks turned whiter than the lather on them. The face of a ghost, the ghost of a man three years dead, was staring over his shoulder into the mirror!

Chapter XVIII

Slaves over the Seas

KNOX whirled around to confront the apparition. The "ghost" was solid flesh, and its tanned features were strikingly familiar. The General let out a great bellow that startled the horses on the picket line.

"Kent!"

He caught his lieutenant in a bear hug that nearly cracked his ribs. As Brooks, who had been similarly greeted by Sergeant Sampson, said later, it would be wise next time to pick a less vigorous welcoming committee.

In answer to Knox's eager volley of questions Andrews poured out his story. Knox listened intently to his lieutenant's account of his capture after Monmouth, his imprisonment in the Sugar House and the escape attempt, and the transfer overseas. But it was the extraordinary adventures of the two artillerymen in the spice islands that held him spellbound.

161

"It was Sumatra the East Indiaman took us to, sir," Andrews said. "Halfway around the world."

"Sumatra!" Knox exclaimed. "Large island south of the Malay Peninsula. We had a map that showed it in the shop in Boston. Island's about a thousand miles long as I remember. Equator runs smack through the middle of it."

"Right, sir, and it's hotter'n blazes. The Dutch hold one end of it and the British the other. When they're not fighting each other, they fight the natives. I guess the spice trade's worth it."

This is the rest of the story Andrews told his commander:

The East Indiaman made port in the harbor of Bencoulen on the east coast of Sumatra. It was a town long held by England.

When the prisoners were allowed on the deck, a scene of grandeur and lush beauty met their eyes. Coastal lowlands were backed by lofty mountain ranges, clothed by thick green forests of oak, camphor, and teak. Here and there among the distant heights smoked the cone-topped peaks of active volcanoes. A shore breeze, wafting the heavy fragrance of tropical flowers, carried also waves of oppressive heat.

Brooks turned away and sighed. "Pretty but I'd trade all that for Boston on a crisp winter day."

Andrews nodded sadly as they joined the rest of the prisoners in boats that took them ashore.

The stronger men among the new arrivals, including Andrews and Brooks, were drafted to serve in the John Company army, to reinforce native soldiers called Sepoys. They were marched out to drill by a tough, grizzled British sergeant.

"You're the lucky lads," the sergeant told them. "Soldier for me and do your duty and you'll have an easy time of it. Sulk on me, and you're for the pepper fields. One day sweatin' there will be all you need to find out you made the mistake of your life—what there is left of it."

Andrews muttered out of the side of his mouth to Brooks. "Just the same I'm not going to soldier for him. I'll not carry arms for the enemy. No more than I would at home when that would have let us out of the Sugar House."

"I'm with you," Brooks whispered. "But what'll we do? If we refuse duty straight out, we'll see the whipping post again."

"You and I," said Andrews, "are going to turn into the most tarnal, awful, awkward squad that the good sergeant here ever met."

From long habit they could not help marching in a military manner at first, but when they were given dummy muskets for instruction in the manual of arms, they put on an exhibition of clumsy juggling that had the sergeant roaring at them in exasperation.

"You two clodhoppers there!" he shouted. "We ought to won the war long ago if you're what the Rebels call soldiers."

Brooks gave him a stupid stare. "But sergeant, sir," he protested. "We wasn't no soldiers. Artill'ry drivers we was. Never did no drillin' or fightin'."

"Never liked neither," Andrews added. "We likes hosses though. Got any 'round here, mister? We'll take good care of 'em for ye."

For an hour more the pair muffed almost every command. They tripped over their muskets and sprawled flat. Brooks, prone, whispered to his companion. "If only Sergeant Sampson could see us now!" At last the raving drillmaster gave up and barked an order to an assistant.

"Double-time these two oafs out of here! Prick 'em with

your bay'net if they don't move fast enough. Turn 'em over to the overseer and tell him to work hell out of 'em."

So from dawn to dark Andrews and Brooks toiled on the pepper plantations. Overseers drove them harshly, and they were alertly guarded by Sepoys. Yet hard, backbreaking labor under a burning sun in the open was far better than the dreadful confinement of the Sugar House. Every night prisoners huddled in their fenced compound to whisper plans for escape. If they could make their way across the island to one of the Dutch forts on the west coast, they might well obtain passage home. Before Andrews was captured he had heard that the Dutch might join France in alliance against Britain to help the United States win independence.

But a convict laborer the prisoners questioned strongly discouraged an attempt at a breakaway. "You'll never make it, mates," he insisted. "I've been here five years and seen what happens to them as tries to fly the coop. They gets shot or stuck like pigs by the Sepoys.

"Say you does give the Sepoys the slip. Nothin' to stop you then but the wild beasts and snakes in them jungles. I seen what was left of some of them that got clear, brought back by trackers to be like a lesson to us. Horrid sights they was. Me, I'm for stayin' right here, and so'll you coves if you don't want to die nasty-like."

Some of the Americans were dissuaded, and others lapsed into hopelessness; as the heat and poor food began to tell on them, numbers sickened and died. Only five, including Andrews and Brooks, kept to their resolution.

Weeks passed before they could steal any weapons, and then they managed to lay hand on knives only. They made bayonets out of them by binding them to staffs. A small store of provisions was accumulated. Andrews also stole fireworks—flint and steel—and slipped them into his pocket. They now had a means to kindle fires to cook their food or warm themselves in the cold of the mountains.

Finally, on a dark night, the five scaled the fence and ran. But a patrol of Sepoys spotted them before they were past the pepper fields. Muskets spurted flame. By their flare Andrews and Brooks saw their companions fall. A group of Sepoys, muskets emptied but bayonets fixed, rushed at the uninjured survivors. The artillerymen lunged with their homemade bayonets as they had seen von Steuben teach the infantry to do at Valley Forge. Two Sepoys screamed and went down. The rest fled. Into the jungle plunged the two escapees. They did not slow their panting run until the hue and cry of pursuit had died away behind them.

After a night during which they were afraid to sleep for fear of the lions, tigers, and panthers of which the convict had warned them, they resolutely began the tremendous journey that lay before them. By a direct line it was 200 miles across the island to the nearest Dutch settlement of Croy, but the distance was 800 miles, traveling along the coast. Without hesitation they chose the latter, not daring to risk the interior route where, if they survived beasts of prey and snakes, they might so easily become lost. Day after day, counted by notching a stick hung around Andrews' neck, they drove themselves onward. They lived on fruit, turtle eggs, and turtle which they cooked over fires, kept burning all night to scare off wild animals. Once, trying a strange fruit that looked like an orange, they poisoned themselves, and three wretched days passed before they were strong enough to resume their march. In a kind of delirium they pushed on, fancying they heard voices calling them, dogs barking, and all the familiar sounds of home. It did not seem strange when a yellow dog loped up to them and rubbed against their legs to be petted.

Andrews, his brain suddenly clearing, cried, "Look out, Eph! That's no dog. It's a lion cub. Likely its mother's near. Come on! Get out of here!"

They turned and ran, the cub gamboling playfully at their heels. Before they had covered a hundred feet, a lioness burst out of the underbrush. Brooks and Andrews faced her, weakly leveling their bayonet staffs, though aware they could make little defense against the charge of the great tawny beast. But the cub ran to its mother, and she laid down before it a piece of meat. As the men cautiously backed away, the lioness roared, and let them go.

Another time they were stalked by a tiger, but again a bold front saved them, and their threatening gestures and loud shouts drove the animal off. Later a whole tribe of chattering apes, baring their teeth and hurling sticks, followed them for miles. Although the creatures fled and climbed into trees when the men turned on them, driving them off cost considerable effort. The two travelers were exhausted and nerve-wracked by nightfall when their tormenters finally left them.

Andrews had cut the one hundred and fifth notch in his stick on the day that he and Brooks, supporting each other, tottered into an Indian village. Its inhabitants, fortunately friendly, fed them rice and goat's milk. In a smattering of Malay he had picked up, Andrews made them understand that he and his companion were trying to reach the Dutch town of Croy which proved to be only three miles farther. Guided and helped by the Indians, they covered the last stage of their journey.

A stolid Dutch skipper gaped at the thin, bearded

scarecrows who staggered up to him, muttering in English and making imploring motions toward his ship, anchored in the harbor.

"We're Americans. Please take us home," Andrews kept repeating.

"Home," Brooks echoed, his voice pleading.

At last the Dutchman spoke. "Amerika? Long voyage. Vell, koom. I giff you a start."

By a succession of vessels, first Dutch and then French, that gave them passage from port to port, the artillerymen sailed back around the world.

"And here we are, sir." Andrews finished. "We landed at Newport and journeyed on here to Jersey. Lieutenant Andrews and Corporal Brooks report for duty."

"A rare and marvelous tale," Henry Knox said. "Almost incredible but, coming from you, I do not doubt a word. We've had vague rumors that the British were shipping prisoners to out-of-the-way places. Your story confirms that. Set it all down in a journal when you find a chance, Kent. Published, it would sell many copies. If you and I go back to selling books after the war—"

"I don't believe we will, sir. War changes men."

"So it does, and we have not finished the war. It's been a long time since 1775." Knox broke off and stared straight at the young officer. "Look here. Do you mean to say you came back to the army without going home first to see your mother and Constancy? Why—"

"Well, sir, Brooks and I sent letters home by the first post to Boston. Then we thought we'd better report to you. As you said, the war isn't over. Perhaps a couple of old artillerymen might be useful—that is, if they weren't setting too much store by themselves."

There was pride and deep affection in the way Knox regarded his lieutenant, but he hid them while he pretended to ponder the matter.

"Yes, it's possible I might make use of you," he said. "Come to think of it, we've a siege train to be moved south. Did you see the French heavy artillery when you were in Newport?"

"Yes, sir. Mortars, howitzers, and guns from twenty-fours down. They're aboard the fleet sailing under Admiral Barras."

"That's easy transportation. We're faced with bad roads. Well, you and Brooks helped me bring the guns from Ticonderoga. Of course we had the cannon on sleds then, with plenty of snow and the rivers frozen. This is a different sort of problem, but you may come in handy.

"Now tell Brooks—Sergeant Brooks as of today—that he's to pick out one of our big mortars that reminds him of 'The Old Sow' and wrestle with it. Let me think what I can do with you, Kent. Can't give you back your three-pounders. They're too light for the work ahead of us. Placing an unattached lieutenant is difficult. There aren't any vacancies for your rank."

The General thought for a while longer, as Andrews, feeling uncomfortably superfluous, waited nervously. At last Knox nodded with the satisfaction of one who solves a knotty riddle and shouted for his aide. When the young man hurried in, Knox told him:

"This returned officer is assigned to the siege train. Find sidearms and borrow a uniform for him." The gray eyes were twinkling, and a broad grin creased the lathered face, as the big man added: "See to it that the uniform has the epaulettes of a captain."

Chapter XIX

Siege Train Southward

CAPTAIN Kent Andrews, riding with the siege guns, kept looking toward the head of the column where the Stars and Stripes fluttered. The sight stirred him as it always had, as it would all his life. Back flooded the memory of the long years in prison and a distant land when he feared he would never again see that beloved banner nor proudly wear this uniform of blue with facings of artillery red. Tap of drums and notes of fifes sounded faintly, almost drowned by the rumbling wheels of gun carriages.

Here rolled such power as had blasted the British out of Boston. Twenty-three iron twenty-four- and eighteen-pounders. Twenty-one brass howitzers and mortars, with the larger calibres among the latter mounted on strong traveling beds, drawn by four- and six-horse teams. Fifteen

169

pieces of field artillery marching with the brigades. Aboard the French fleet in Newport, Andrews had counted twenty or more heavy siege guns, ranging from thirteen-inch mortars down to long eighteens. Only in forts like Louisbourg and Ticonderoga had the New World seen such a mighty assemblage of ordnance. Andrews was reminded of the words of an old English chronicler in a book in the Boston shop, a boast that the array of artillery mustered by Henry VIII—great bombards, culverins, falconets, and basilisks— were "cannon enough to conquer Hell." Well, the American and French siege guns could make a hell of any town or stronghold a certain general of George III might try to hold—that is, if Cornwallis could be brought to bay.

The whole campaign depended upon "ifs"—too many of them, Andrews reflected worriedly. *If* Clinton did not sally forth from New York and intercept the southward march of the American and French columns. *If* Lafayette and his few troops could keep Cornwallis in check until Washington and Rochambeau arrived. *If* De Grasse from the West Indies and Barras from Newport succeeded in evading or fighting off the three British fleets at sea. *If*— and this loomed large to the new captain of artillery concerned with it—this heavy siege train could make the long, hard march to Virginia.

Carriages broke down under their weight of metal or overturned in the rutted roads. Poles and traces snapped. Scarcely a mile was covered without weary artillerymen being forced to man dragropes and strain at wheel spokes to help the struggling horses. When New Jersey lay behind them, the danger from Clinton was past for the time being; but as they pushed deeper into Pennsylvania, driving for Williamsburg, Virginia, the autumn days grew sultry, and men and animals wilted in the heat. At the halts Andrews, who had harnessed his horse in to help a team as Hamilton did at Trenton, flung himself down, dripping and panting, beside Brooks, Sampson, and their mortar crews. They all realized now that if they brought these guns through, it would be a feat second only to their winter journey from Fort Ti to Dorchester Heights.

Mile after mile, day after day. Andrews was too tired to count them even by notching a stick as he had in Sumatra. All that mattered was to keep the guns rolling and not let General Knox down. It was said that Washington had recommended his Chief of Artillery to Congress for a major-generalcy. Every artilleryman, from the youngest matross to the oldest veteran, was determined that promotion must go through.

Pushing into Virginia and turning east toward the coast, they made park in sight of York River, flowing into Chesapeake Bay. Cheers from up ahead told them that the long march—one of the fastest in history—was over, and that they were united with Lafayette's troops. Yonder on a bluff on the south side of the river Andrews saw a town. Encircling it and stretching out toward him was a series of formidable-looking earthworks, with cannon peering from their embrasures.

Andrews found an old friend, an officer of Wayne's Pennsylvanians, brigaded with Lafayette's army, and questioned him excitedly.

"Yep, that's old Cornwallis and about seven thousand Britishers and Hessians bottled up there in Yorktown," the other answered jubilantly. "They're on a peninsula, and now that you boys and the French are here, we've got the bottle corked. Can't get out to save 'em. Old Corny's got only a few ships in the river. Guess he figures a British fleet'll sail in and take him off. One already tried to, but it came smack up against Admiral De Grasse, blockading the Bay, and he gave them a proper licking."

The Pennsylvanian looked over the siege train admiringly and exclaimed, "Man, you brought along some heavy metal, and can we use it! Those British earthworks would be tough for infantry to storm. Cornwallis had two thousand Negro slaves building them. Pound those forts and the town to pieces for us, will you? You might begin on that one." He pointed to a star-shaped redoubt jutting out from the first line of entrenchments and added, "It's strongly held. Called the Fusiliers' Redoubt."

Andrews gave a sudden start. "Fusiliers? What Fusiliers?"

"The Royal Welch. Hard-fighting outfit. Ever come up against 'em?"

Andrews nodded grimly. "Certainly have. They chased us off Bunker Hill. Drove us at Brandywine, too."

Wayne's officer grinned. "Your turn this time, Kent. Blast 'em out of there."

Had David Thorpe survived the war? If he had, surely he was commanding a platoon or company in the redoubt over there. This time there could be no impulse of mercy for the one-time friend he had seen over gun sights at Bunker Hill. Andrews felt an unexpected twinge of sadness. A gallant soldier, that rival of his. Of course, Thorpe had tried to win Constancy from him, but could he be blamed for that? Andrews had long since ceased to suspect that Thorpe had anything to do with spiriting the girl away from Boston on the brigantine. He glanced toward his mortars. He would have no qualms about directing their fire on the Fusiliers' Redoubt, but he was glad that the long-range bombardment would be an impersonal affair. Enemy though Thorpe was, Andrews could not feel toward him the hatred those brutal jailers, Cunningham and O'Keefe, had aroused in him.

He was still more relieved after trenches were dug and gun emplacements were built. The Fusiliers' Redoubt lay in the French artillery's sector. Yet he was seized by a premonition that he and David Thorpe would meet in combat.

"The officers of Artillery in the Batteries are to level every piece themselves."

Obeying that order of General Knox's, officers of Colonel Lamb's 2nd Continental and others of detachments of the 4th and 1st carefully sighted along gun barrels or figured angles of fire for mortars and howitzers. Ranges from the emplacements in the American trenches, dug to parallel the British, were from 800 to 1200 yards, and the effect of cannon balls and shells on the enemy redoubts and houses of the town could easily be observed. On October 9th, 1781, gunners stood by with lighted matches, awaiting the order to fire.

Andrews had just finished laying Brooks' mortar when he straightened up to find Knox behind him, and beside the Chief of Artillery stood General Washington himself.

"Your target, Captain?" Knox demanded, as Andrews stiffened to attention.

"That house over there in Yorktown, sir." Andrews pointed. "Spyglass shows officers often entering it. It's probably a staff headquarters."

"Good target." Knox turned to address Washington. "Your Excellency, these are the two escaped prisoners I told you of, Captain Andrews and Sergeant Brooks. Will you do them the honor of opening the bombardment by firing the first shot from their mortar?"

Washington smiled warmly. "It's a long way home from

the spice islands," he said. "I'd like them to feel their travel was not in vain. Sergeant, your match."

Brooks, beaming, handed over the smoldering linstock. While Andrews watched nervously—was his aim true, was the fuse cut to the proper length?—as the Commander touched the flame to the primer in the vent.

The mortar bellowed. Its shell, fuse smoking, soared steeply into the sky, curved down from the top of its trajectory, smashed through the roof of the house, and burst with a blast that made timber fly.

"May all our guns be as well served!" Washington's praise had barely been spoken when with a mighty crash fifty pieces along the American and French front drowned the echoes of that first shot. British cannon, most of them ship's guns taken from one of the frigates in the river, roared back. But the Allied guns and gunnery were overwhelmingly superior. Shells plunged down on enemy parapets and, exploding, flung up cascades of earth and mangled bodies. Some "overs" that missed the town burst in the river to send waterspouts surging high, but so many houses were hit that Cornwallis, shelled out of his headquarters, was forced to move into a tent. French artillery found the range of one of the British frigates and poured red-hot round shot into her. Wrapped in a torrent of fire, she burned to the waterline. Yet French infantry, assaulting the Fusiliers' Redoubt, was strongly repulsed.

The cannonade thundered on. By day the shells, crossing each other's paths, were smoking black balls; by night blazing meteors with crimson tails. Andrews heard Brooks at his mortar loudly declaiming Shakespeare:

Fierce fiery warriors fight upon the clouds,
In ranks and squadrons and right form of war . . .

while Sergeant Sampson shouted his old protest, "Close your trap, Eph. You gabble worse'n ever since you come back."

With scarcely a respite the Allied batteries pounded the British forts, smashing guns and carriages in the embrasures, blowing up magazines. The rate of fire rose to an even more rapid tempo, as powder-grimed crews flung themselves on their guns to swab, load, and fire again. Andrews was filled with pride that day he heard General Lafayette enthusiastically telling a major behind him, "We fire faster than the French. Upon my honor I speak the truth. American artillery—one of the wonders of the Revolution."

Now Cornwallis was forced to pull in his defenses, and the circle tightened around him. American and French columns stormed two British redoubts, and the guns of the Allies moved up to emplacements in new lines of trenches. There, at the deadly range of 400 yards, they poured a devastating stream of iron on the cramped and crowded enemy. All the British guns but one mortar and a few small coehorns were silenced.

Doggedly Cornwallis held out. A fleet, sailing down from New York to break the French blockade, could still save him. He must buy time.

On the night of October 16th assault troops, led by three hundred and fifty Royal Welch Fusiliers, sallied out in a sortie against forward batteries of the American and French, determined to put some of those terrible cannon out of action.

Storming parties dashed forward over the few hundred yards of shell-torn ground between the lines. Muskets flamed along the Allied front, but the assault closed ranks and never faltered. Bayonets gleaming in the moonlight, the grenadiers and light infantry surged on without firing a shot.

"Up the Fusiliers!" Big men in scarlet scaled the parapets or forced their way through the gun embrasures. Desperate fights raged in the crowded trenches—bayonets and musket butts against rammer staffs, handspikes, and pistols. In that confused struggle within the earthworks, combatants could be distinguished only by the shape of their headgear, looming in the shadows. Irresistibly the tide of tall bearskins of the Fusiliers and smaller caps of the light infantry broke the dam of Continental tricornes —and swept them back into the connecting and support trenches. Over in the French sector rallying shouts of "*Vive le Roi!*" receded and grew fainter. There, too, the storm troops had carried the redoubt.

Andrews, both sword and pistol lost in the melee, leaned panting against the wall of an approach trench. As soon as he and his men caught their breath, he must lead a countercharge to recapture the guns. Reinforcements were hurrying in from the flanks and rear. He groped for a weapon. His hand closed on a bayoneted musket, dropped by a sentry.

"Sampson, Brooks, all of you," he called. "Get ready to follow me."

"Right with you, sir."

Before they could advance, a light—a torch or a fire kindled to destroy a gun carriage—flared up ahead in the redoubt they had lost. The Americans saw Fusiliers hammering bayonets into the vents of the cannon, spiking them.

Sergeant Sampson bellowed with rage. Flourishing a

club—part of a broken rammer staff—he charged alone.

Andrews and the others yelled and rushed after him. They were still yards behind when a British officer stepped into the entrance of the redoubt. The light revealed him clearly. Beyond a doubt it was David Thorpe. Steadily he leveled a musket and fired. Sampson flung up his arms, staggered, and dropped in a still heap.

Wild, blazing fury seized Andrews. He leaped over the body of his comrade. Bayonet outthrust, he hurled himself at Thorpe in a headlong lunge. The Fusilier parried with all his strength. Andrews' blade slid past. Carried on by the impetus of his charge and knocked off balance by the parry, he crashed to the ground. As he scrambled to his knees, Thorpe swung the butt of his musket at his jaw. With a sudden jerk the American dodged. The blow grazed his head, ripping an ear. His hands slid up the barrel of his gun to a grip close under its fixed bayonet. Then he heaved himself to his feet and jabbed upward, feeling his blade drive in, hearing his enemy groan. An onrush of men from behind jostled him aside. Faint and sickened, he leaned on his musket and watched the British, still fighting stubbornly, driven from the redoubt. But their sortie had partly achieved its objective. They left three of the American cannon and two of the French spiked.

But already artificers were at work, bending over the breeches. The bayonets the Fusiliers had used were by no means as effective as regular spiking irons which could be pounded down into vents so that they had to be drilled out. It did not take long to wrench the bayonets loose. Soon Brooks was reporting to his captain. "Mortars ready for action again, sir."

"Very well. Open fire." After giving the order Andrews

said sadly, "I'm going back to see that Sampson's body is taken care of. Tell Corporal Sims he's in command of the other piece."

Back in the approach trench Andrews met a surgeon who had just come up and was bending over Sampson's still form. He looked up to say:

"Sounded like a hot fight, Captain, but I'm told this man was the only one killed on our side, Too bad. Fine, big fellow. Well, it only takes one slug of lead in the right place. Shot through the heart or near it. Sergeant of yours, you say? . . . Know how you must feel. British carried off their wounded, didn't they? Well . . ." With a perfunctory gesture the surgeon grasped a wrist to take the pulse. Suddenly he straightened up. "Captain, bring stretcher-bearers! There's still life in this man!"

A drummer boy climbed on top of a battered British parapet and stood there, sticks flailing away at his drumhead. In the din of the bombardment he might have been a figure in a pantomime. A sergeant appeared beside him, waving a white flag. Then the guns ceased firing, and in the sudden, startling silence the drummer's signal sounded clear. He was beating the parley.

Cheers rang out along the Allied lines. Cornwallis must be asking for terms of surrender. A parley could mean nothing else. His defenses were shattered, his sorties repulsed, his attempt to escape across the river had failed. He must give up, or be blown to bits.

Washington demanded the surrender of the cornered British army, its arms, and colors on October 19th, nor would he brook delay, for a relieving fleet might still arrive at any moment. Cornwallis could only accept. Meanwhile the victors sent food to the hungry garrison and surgeons to help care for the many wounded in Yorktown.

When Andrews heard that American doctors were going through the lines, he was sitting at the bedside of Sergeant Sampson, who was making a splendid recovery.

"Sergeant," he asked, "do you mind if I go over and see what happend to that Fusilier officer that shot you? If he'd done for you, he could be dead for all I'd care. But you're going to get well, and he was a friend of mine in Boston before the war."

"Go ahead, sir," Sampson answered. "No hard feelings now. We've licked 'em. 'Sides, from what Eph says, you fixed that Lobster-back proper."

"I did my best to, but—well, I've got to know."

Andrews found David Thorpe in a hospital established in a half-ruined house. He looked down into the Fusilier's pale face.

"I tried to kill you, David," he said.

Thorpe smiled wanly. "I seem to remember having rather unfriendly designs toward you, Kent."

"You see, I thought you'd killed my sergeant."

"Oh, the big chap with the club who charged me. Then I only wounded him, did I? I'm happy now that was all. He's going to be all right?"

"Yes, but you . . ."

"Yes, so will I. For an artilleryman you're rather good with the bayonet. Of course that first lunge of yours was too precipitate, but the jab was first rate. Missed my lung, though."

"I can't tell you how glad I am."

"I believe you, old friend. I can call you that now. We're beaten." Thorpe grinned up from his cot. "Took the French to help you do it. Anyway the war's over. Oh, Clinton may hold out in New York for a while, but it's really ended. As soon as I'm in good enough shape and am paroled . . ."

"David, I'll do all I can for you. I've brought food and one of our best surgeons."

"All my thanks. I'll be going home in a hospital ship and . . ." The wounded man smiled again and winked. "And I'll promise you something. I won't try to land in Boston to be nursed by a young lady we know. Got me nowhere last time. Best of luck to you, Kent."

With bands playing but colors furled and sheathed, the British army marched out of shattered Yorktown. The long column filed between lines of the conquerors, drawn up opposite each other. Over the French regiments in gleaming white waved their gorgeous regimental colors. The Stars and Stripes floated free above ranks in Continental blue and brown, uniforms often threadbare and ragged but worn proudly.

What was that tune the British fifers were playing? *The World Turned Upside Down*. Broad grins, approving the choice of music, broke out along the lines. But Lafayette was ready with an answer to leave King George's men no doubt about who had upset the world for them. He ordered American fifes to strike up *Yankee Doodle*. Its lively strains, once defiant, now triumphant, shrilled loud and clear.

A British general, deputy for Cornwallis who had reported he was sick, rode forward to surrender his sword to the French instead of to the upstart Rebels. Instantly Rochambeau waved him toward Washington. On flowed the long scarlet column, halting, sullenly flinging down arms on a high-mounting heap, moving dispiritedly on to prison camps. Defeat, surrender, to be prisoners of war—a bitter cup to drain. In the ranks of the American artillery a captain and a sergeant watched with sympathy they could not repress.

Drums beat dismissal. Andrews, ordered to report to General Knox, found his chief beaming happily.

"A great day!" Knox exclaimed. "A courier's riding with the news to Mount Vernon. Lucy's there, you know, staying with Mistress Washington."

"Pray present my affectionate regards, sir."

"Gladly. Well, duty calls. We're still fighting a war. On to New York next. My headquarters will be at West Point. You are to command a battery there."

"Thank you, sir."

"Meanwhile a convoy of wounded is going north via Philadelphia. If Sergeant Sampson is well enough to travel, see that he's in it. Sergeant Brooks is to go along to take care of him."

"Very good, sir. Anything further?"

"Yes. You will have charge of the convoy, Captain Andrews. Take the Massachusetts men on to their homes. On reaching Boston if you see anyone I know, pray present *my* affectionate regards."

CHAPTER XX

A Gun Goes Home

MAJOR Kent Andrews, stationed at the School of Instruction later to be called the United States Military Academy, at West Point, took leave in the summer of 1795. His purpose was to visit Major-General Henry Knox, who had retired a year before as Secretary of War and moved to Maine.

At the rail of a packet, sailing down the Hudson to New York, Andrews looked forward to his visit with eager anticipation. It was high honor for any man to be General Knox's guest. Every American owed much to Washington's wartime Chief of Artillery whose great services had not ended with the Revolution in '83. The new school, astern there on the Highlands, had been his idea. As Secretary of War he had done all he could to promote the country's defense, organizing a militia system, helping to strengthen the navy. It was he who had banded together Washington's ex-officers in the Order of the Cincinnati, to keep alive the spirit of patriotism and loyalty that had won independence. Springfield Arsenal, established during the war, was another of his monuments. Though Knox now had left the cabinet of President Washington, he had by no means retired, but was busy with many enterprises on the vast Maine estate Lucy had inherited from her grandfather, General Waldo.

Andrews, staring down the river toward New York, was lost in memories. Could it be so long as twelve years ago that the British had evacuated the city, and his battery had marched in, part of the army proudly led by General Knox?

He felt a warm presence at the rail beside him and heard his wife's soft voice merrily demanding, "Kent! Come back with those thoughts of yours! You're off in the war again."

"Guess I was, Constancy. A habit of old soldiers." He smiled down into her glowing face.

"I know, Major. But it's high time you helped stand sentry over the children. Your two sons are a handful, and your small daughter, Lucy, hardly less. They're all so excited about this trip. A kind sailor is watching them now, but you'd best relieve him soon. They've worn me out already."

"As you order, ma'am."

"And here's another order, sir. When we get to Maine, you simply must not spend all the time fighting the war over with General Knox."

"But the General likes to . . ."

"Don't I remember! But you have your duty to the ladies."

"But the surprise we're bringing from New York. That's going to recall the war aplenty."

"I've allowed for that. Will it be ready?"

"Certainly. Lieutenant Brooks and Sergeant Sampson are seeing to it. They'll meet us in New York at the dock where we board the schooner for Maine.

"Eph Brooks makes a good officer," Constancy said, "but I've never understood why Sampson was content to stay in the ranks."

"He'd never consider a commission. He's one of those grand old non-coms who are the backbone of the army, and he doesn't want to be anything else. Only thing that comes hard to him, I guess, is not being able to tell his lieutenant, 'Close your trap, Eph!'" Andrews grinned. "Maybe, off duty, he still does."

He went to find the children, wondering whether young Kent and Waite would join the artillery when they grew up. There wasn't much left of the army right now, but in time it would come back to strength. Meanwhile he was proud as always to wear the uniform. He could still remember his lost, uncomfortable feeling during '84 when the reduction of the Army to a mere handful of men had forced him into civilian clothes and pursuits for a while.

At the New York water front he found Brooks and Sampson, along with a gunner and four matrosses from his old battery. As he approached, they straightened to attention and saluted formally, but in their eyes shone the pleasure of a meeting between old comrades-in-arms. Andrews returned the salute, then clasped the hands of his fellow veterans.

"Freight aboard, sir, and stowed below," Brooks reported. "Everything covered with tarpaulins. Even if General Knox looked into the hold, he couldn't tell what we're bringing him."

"Good. And your uniforms?"

"In our kit bags. We understand that we're not to put them on till you give the order, Major."

"What's hidden down in the ship, Father?" demanded three curious young voices almost at once.

"A carriage and some other old things," Andrews answered. At the first opportunity he drew the men aside and whispered:

"Keep the hatches battened down. It seems we have three small spies aboard. If they get wind of the General's surprise, it will be no surprise at all."

After a fair voyage along the coast to Maine, the schooner sailed into Penobscot Bay and made her way up the St. George's River to the little village of Thomaston. There rose the gleaming white walls of the Knox mansion, "Montpelier." Stately and spacious with its two stories, it seemed the embodiment of hospitality. Indeed five hundred people had been entertained there last July 4th at the housewarming. As the schooner glided toward the wharf, evidences of Knox's activities were displayed: ships building in a yard, barges loaded with farm produce, lumber, and quarried stone.

The heartiest of welcomes awaited the travelers. The bulky, robust General, over three hundred pounds now, crushed hands and pounded backs in greeting. Lucy, tall and more imposing than ever, bent low to take Constancy in her arms, while her daughters, Lucy and Caroline, knelt to hug the children. Escorted into the mansion, Constancy exclaimed in rapture over the marvelous flying staircase, its twin flights bathed in sun from a skylight, seeming to hang suspended in luminous air; the lovely oval room, the dining room, the library with its sixteen hundred volumes; the charming guest room assigned her and her husband, with a nursery next door for the children. Pails of hot water stood ready beside a portable bathtub which, a maid said, had been the General's own. Constancy smiled gratefully but with amusement. No wonder the General had needed a new tub; he must have bulged out of this one.

After dinner that night, Brooks brought Sampson from the brick bachelor quarters near the mansion to meet Major Andrews privately on the porch.

"Orders, sir?" Brooks asked.

"Unload the freight quietly tonight," Andrews directed. "Hide it behind the wharf shed, all except the harness. Take that to the stables. The General has twenty-six horses, riding and carriage. I've arranged for mounts for us tomorrow. I said we'd like to ride over part of the estate. We can take any horse we want, just so we don't touch Mrs. Knox's. The General tried to borrow it once for a guest and got his comeuppance. He told me he had to call the groom and order him, 'John, put Mrs. Knox's horse back in the stable and don't take it out again until God Almighty or Mrs. Knox tells you!'"

The other two laughed. Undoubtedly there were times when Mistress Lucy ranked her major-general.

Andrews spoke on. "Tomorrow morning my wife will keep our host and hostess occupied indoors. At nine o'clock, in uniform, lead the horses to the wharf shed, harness and hitch."

"If we don't give General and Mrs. Knox the surprise of their lives," Brooks said, his voice rising in excitement, "I'll go jump in the river. Why we'll . . ."

"Close your trap, Eph," Andrews interrupted, grinning.

"Thank you, sir," said Sergeant Sampson. "The Major took the words out of my mouth."

Up the driveway to "Montpelier" next morning rolled a half section of artillery. Major Andrews rode at its head, his lieutenant to his left rear. A four-horse team in pairs, with two matrosses as drivers on the near animals, pulled a limber with a glistening bronze three-pounder hooked to the pintle. Behind rode Sergeant Sampson, his gunner, and the two other matrosses.

General Knox strode out onto the porch to beam fondly at the familiar spectacle: the trim fieldpiece and the riders in Continental blue with the scarlet facings of the artillery. Then he began to gape.

"By thunder!" he cried. "The whole crew's mounted. Why that's a flying battery. That's the horse artillery the French artillerist, Gribeauval, has been developing. Kent got his idea from there of course. Right, Constancy?"

"Yes, General," she answered delightedly.

"Artillery like that can get where it's needed in a hurry," Knox rushed on. "It can support cavalry. Our army must adopt it. If I were still Secretary of War . . ."

Andrews shouted an order. The gun crew dismounted, turned their mounts over to the still-mounted drivers, unlimbered, loaded, primed, and fired a salute.

Knox hurried down to congratulate the artillerymen. He slapped the barrel of the smoking gun. "This ought to be a six-pounder though," he said.

"Should be, General," Andrews agreed, "but not this time. Look closely at the breech, sir. Marking's faint but it can still be read."

Knox stared down. "It's 'Mistress Lucy'!" he roared in his great voice.

"The British took her to New York after they captured her on Long Island," Andrews explained. "When they evacuated the city, they hid her. A little while ago she was found, and the War Department gave permission to bring her to you."

The General's gray eyes were bright with happiness. A gun had come home.

Author's Postscript

Many books furnished the background for this story. I shall mention only some of the chief ones. They include:

Biographies of Henry Knox by Noah Brooks, Francis S. Drake, and North Callahan

Douglas Southall Freeman's *George Washington*

General histories of the Revolution by Sir George Otto Trevelyn, F. V. Greene, Allen French, Christopher Ward, and Lynn Montross

Stephen Bonsal's *When the French Were Here*

Battle studies by Alfred Hoyt Bill, William S. Stryker, and Colonel H. L. Landers

Alexander C. Flick's account of Knox and the Ticonderoga guns, in *Proceedings and Quarterly Journal*, New York State Historical Association, vol. 9 (1928)

Treatises on artillery by John Müller, William Stevens, and Louis de Tousard

William E. Birkhimer's *Historical Sketch of the Artillery, U.S. Army*

My own *Sound of the Guns*

The Journal of John Blatchford in Danske Dandridge's *American Prisoners of the Revolution*, on which the transportation of Andrews and Brooks to Sumatra and their escape are based.

      *   *   *

The guns, "Hancock" and "Adams," continued in action throughout the Revolution. They were so named, Callahan states, when Henry Knox was Secretary of War. By his order each was decorated with a plate reading:

189

> This is one of the four cannon
> Which constituted the whole train
> of field artillery possessed by
> The British Colonies of North America
> At the commencement of the war,
> On the 19th of April, 1775.
> This cannon and its fellow, belonging
> To a number of citizens of Boston.
> The other two, the property of the
> Government of Massachusetts,
> Were taken by the enemy.

When the Bunker Hill Monument was built, both guns were given an honored place in its top chamber.

The names of "Mistress Lucy," "Saint Paul," and "Frederick the Great," have been given to three-pounders whose names are not recorded.

Among the patriots who hid the guns in the schoolhouse were Samuel Gore and William Dawes. The latter made the midnight ride to Lexington along with Revere and Prescott.

I could not discover the identity of the gun Molly Pitcher helped serve at Monmouth, so I availed myself of the novelist's privilege and assigned it to Andrews' battery. This also was the case with the piece from which General Washington fired the first shot at Yorktown.

Introduction of horse artillery, with the cannoneers all mounted, in the last chapter is premature historically. The first American regiment of that type was not organized until 1808. However, it may have developed from beginnings such as Andrews staged when he presented "Mistress Lucy" to Knox in Maine.

* * *

I am happy to acknowledge my debt for help in the writing of this book to the following: the late Colonel Harry C. Larter, Jr., an expert on the gunnery, uniforms, and equipment of the Revolution; Harold L. Peterson and Henry I. Shaw, Jr., of the Company of Military Collectors & Historians; Oliver G. Swan, of Paul R. Reynolds & Son, my literary agents; my wife, Mildred

Adams Downey, for her criticism and the typing of most of this novel, as of my previous thirty-four books.

FAIRFAX DOWNEY
West Springfield, New Hampshire,
1961